DREAMTIME

DREAMTIME

A Collection of Short Stories

Robert F. Steiner

iUniverse Star
New York Lincoln Shanghai

Dreamtime

A Collection of Short Stories

Copyright © 2004, 2007 by Robert Steiner

iUniverse books may be ordered through booksellers or by contacting:

iUniverse
2021 Pine Lake Road, Suite 100
Lincoln, NE 68512
www.iuniverse.com
1-800-Authors (1-800-288-4677)

This is a work of fiction. All of the characters, names, incidents, organizations, and dialogue in this novel are either the products of the author's imagination or are used fictitiously.

ISBN-13: 978-1-58348-480-7 (pbk)
ISBN-13: 978-0-595-88207-6 (ebk)
ISBN-10: 1-58348-480-9 (pbk)
ISBN-10: 0-595-88207-2 (ebk)

Printed in the United States of America

CONTENTS

▼

Preface vii

The Decoy 1

The Hiker's Tale: At Anton's Restaurant... 17

The Student Pilot..24

Canine Fantasies 30

The Returning Student 44

The Disappearance..55

Phoenix Street..63

The Seaside Witch 68

The Uninvited Guest 77

The Pilgrim..90

Round Trip.. 105

Preface

"Dreamtime" is the Australian aborigine term for the magical period of the creation of the world. It is reflected in these stories—tales that lie on the borderline of the supernatural. Many involve dreams.

This is least pronounced in the first two stories, both of which are strongly influenced by personal experiences. "The Decoy" stems from an unpleasant occurrence during a trip to Italy in 1995. The story describes the adventures of an unusually ugly young American, who finds that his bizarre appearance is an asset in solving a persistent problem of Italian tourism. In the process he also solves his primary personal problems. "The Hiker's Tale" was inspired by many years of hiking on the beautiful Chesapeake and Ohio towpath, which parallels the Potomac for over a hundred miles. The narrator is trapped in an unpredicted blizzard. The vision experienced by the narrator can be interpreted either literally or as a product of the delirium of a man perishing from hypothermia.

"The Student Pilot" deals with the reincarnation in a contemporary situation of a famous Renaissance artist with an ancillary interest in science and aviation. The flight school parts are as realistic as I can make them. "Canine Fantasies" describes the insertion of a magnificent imaginary dog into the narrator's consciousness as a result of a hypnosis session gone astray. The dog, unperceived by anyone else, comes to dominate the life of the narrator more and more.

Like "The Student Pilot, " "The Returning Student" deals with the return of a great man to terrestrial life, in this case as a part-time student in a second-rate university. The student is a famous poet with a latent fascination for science that was frustrated in his life and which he longs to gratify, even briefly. "The Disappearance" describes a possible example of the Rapture, in which a deserving mortal is snatched away prematurely to the next world. In this case, the man seems to disappear from a tour boat visiting the Great Australian Barrier Reef off Cairns.

He seems to reappear and disappear again much later under puzzling circumstances.

"Phoenix Street," in which dream and reality overlap, tells of the borderline supernatural experience of a Harvard graduate student, although it can also be interpreted as a purely psychological overreaction. "The Seaside Witch" draws on a personal experience of the author during a trip to the Maryland seashore in 1960. The "witch" really existed and is accurately described. Her cottage was carried out to sea in the great storm of 1967. The rescue from the quicksand is also true to life. (Although I have trouble getting people to believe it.)

"The Uninvited Guest" tells of a young Johns Hopkins graduate student who gets lost in 1980 on a dark night while returning to Baltimore from Pennsylvania. He stumbles upon an ornate mansion where he hopes to get directions. He follows a group inside, where a very upscale party is going on to celebrate the election of Ronald Reagan. The guests seem unaware of his presence and he cannot draw their attention. Their conversation is very bizarre and expresses sentiments of extreme reaction. At midnight, they change back to rats.

In "The Pilgrim" I employ a literary device which describes the dream of a man at the moment of death. In my story the central character seems to travel through his life in reverse, beginning at the hospital acute care unit, passing through the places where he has worked and lived, growing ever younger, and ending at his birth. At the end he is guided into the next world by a famous English evangelical writer. Meanwhile, in real time, his daughter is waiting by his bedside in the hospital.

"Round Trip" deals with an unsuccessful space voyage in which the crew is forced to return to Earth after a time lapse of forty years. During this time, America has changed drastically. Among other things, mutations have created new and dangerous forms of microorganisms against which the returnees' immunity has faded. This is a story where I cannot draw on personal experience. I have therefore chosen to narrate it in the third person.

This collection of short stories has been culled from previous books. Many have been independently published in literary magazines since their original appearance and have been subject to editorial modification.

"The Decoy" and "The Returning Student" have been presented in *Words of Wisdom*, "The Hiker's Tale" in *Potomac Review*; "Phoenix Street" and "Canine Fantasies" in *Dream Fantasy International*, and "The Pilgrim" and "The Student Pilot" in *Dandelion Arts Magazine*.

THE DECOY

As I expected, my parents were disturbed about the adventure I was planning, which they had learned of only after I was irrevocably committed. My mother disliked the whole idea.

"It sounds very dangerous to me. You'll be lucky not to get your throat cut. You're just not experienced enough to handle that kind of situation. Are you sure you can't get out of it?"

My father took a somewhat more positive view.

"He's twenty-two years old, for God's sake. Don't sell him short. I think he can handle it."

However, I could tell he was worried.

It began innocuously enough with my answer to an ad in the *Washington Post*. I had just finished my senior year at Georgetown and planned to enter graduate school in the fall. There remained three summer months to get through. I could, of course, simply get some kind of second-rate job to tide me over until classes and my teaching fellowship began. However, what my soul yearned for was to go abroad, especially to Europe. I had never been outside the country and had always been fascinated with all things foreign.

Nevertheless, it seemed hopeless. In order to travel at all, even if roughing it, one needs some minimal amount of money, which I could not even approach. My parents were oppressed by heavy medical expenses that left them severely in debt. I myself had a tuition loan to pay off. So I sighed and resigned myself to another miserable Washington summer. Perhaps when I finished school, if I ever did, and began to have some positive cash flow, I could start to see the world. But how far in the future would that be?

I had put thoughts of foreign travel aside and was perusing the want ads in search of an acceptable summer job when a quarter-page ad seized my attention.

College Graduates!

Applications are invited for a summer position in Italy with the Ministry of Tourism. Ample opportunities to see famous cities. All travel and living expenses paid, plus up to $3000 a month, depending upon qualifications. Knowledge of Italian unnecessary. Unmarried males over 21 only.

The ad went on to cite an address I could write to for application forms, but it gave no further details about the job. I duly wrote away for the forms, filled them out, and returned them, although without much hope. Assuming that it was not some kind of scam, the job seemed too good to be true and would surely attract a multitude of applicants. The forms were unusually detailed and included a number of questions that seemed to comprise a psychological evaluation, including an internal test for self-consistency. A full-length photograph was also required, as well as several references.

My spirits sank when I saw the requirement for a photograph; so much so that I was tempted to abandon the project, for by no stretch of the imagination could my appearance be described as an asset. Indeed, I must have been one of the ugliest men in America. However, I was ugly in a very special way. It was not a question of scarred or deformed features, but of inappropriate proportions. The lower half of my head was too large relative to the upper half, so that it appeared to taper upward. My eyes were too small and set too close together, and my mouth and jaw were much too large and slack. As if that were not enough, I was substantially overweight, especially below the waist. The overall impression was of stupidity and vacuity. In an interview I could hope to offset this by intelligent conversation, but a static photograph did not allow this option.

It was much to my surprise, therefore, when I received an early phone call inviting me to present myself at the local American office of the Tourism Ministry on the following Tuesday at 10:00 AM. I wondered if a mistake had been made but wasted no time in agreeing to come. The three days until Tuesday passed with agonizing slowness. Meanwhile I was offered a job as a counselor at a summer camp for disturbed children but temporized.

I arrived promptly at 10:00 AM but found several others still ahead of me in the waiting room. Before my turn came, I had ample time to study my competition, which grew by three more while I was waiting. I was both gratified and a lit-tle alarmed to observe that they were all of my general physical type and, in fact, somewhat resembled me, so much so that we could have been members of the same extended family. Beyond this, the resemblance faded. The group included both somewhat dim and very sharp young men, as well as both seemingly placid and aggressive individuals.

I was forced to the speculation that my appearance, which I had thought to be a liability, might well be my primary asset. But this made no sense at all, and I was still musing over the alternative possibilities when my name was called, ahead of most of those who had been waiting. This was a good sign. I did not mind the angry glances I drew from the other candidates who had been bypassed.

I was ushered into the interview office where I was greeted by Signor Testa, an elegantly dressed silver-haired man in later middle age who looked rather like Vittorio de Sica. He got to the point at once.

"Mr. Mosby, we have invited you for an interview because your qualifications seem admirably suited to our needs. Perhaps I had better begin by describing the nature of the job, since it is clearly not for everyone. The Italian tourist business, upon which much of our prosperity depends, has been for some time beset by certain problems shared by most of Europe, but they are particularly acute in our country. I am referring to the presence of numerous individuals who have made a profession of preying upon foreign tourists. Their activities take various forms. At one extreme we have gangs of young people who snatch purses, wallets, or money belts after falling unexpectedly upon solitary tourists. At a somewhat more sophisticated level, we have those who lure tourists into some form of putative scam in which they are promised something for nothing and get nothing for something. Finally, we have the most serious case, where tourists are drawn by the promise of some exotic forbidden fruit, such as ancient Roman pornography, and then kidnapped and held for exorbitant ransom."

Although I had never traveled abroad, none of this came as news to me. Stories of victimized tourists were commonplace in the papers. A classmate of mine had been relieved of his wallet, his passport, and all his money in Naples. The period was the early '90s, a time of trouble in the Balkans, Russia, and elsewhere. Signor Testa continued:

"The problem has become so serious that the Tourism Ministry has decided decisive countermeasures are necessary. Since we cannot afford to put swarms of policemen on every street, we have decided to resort to undercover methods, but of an unusual kind. In brief, we plan to place agents at particularly dangerous points in our main cities. These agents are intended to attract predators, to serve as decoys, as it were."

My alarm at hearing this must have shown on my face, for Testa hastened to reassure me.

"Please do not reject the idea out of hand, Signor Mosby. I will not pretend that the element of danger is entirely absent, but it is minimal. You will be by no means defenseless, as you will see. The fact that the risk, while small, cannot be said to be zero, is in part responsible for the high salary and generous perquisites of the position."

"Purely out of curiosity," I asked, "why was I chosen out of the doubtlessly large number of applicants?"

"May I speak freely?" asked Testa. I nodded, despite a sinking feeling.

"Of all kinds of tourist, by far the most attractive to predators are individuals who appear vulnerable, either because of isolation, incapacity, or dullness. Forgive me, but externally you convey an impression of semi-comatose stupidity. You look as though you were daydreaming. I hasten to add that your other data tend to contradict this. They seem to indicate an alert person of above-average intelligence. Both qualities are desirable. We would not want a real fool, only someone who looks like one."

I felt somewhat exasperated, although I had of course asked for it. My feelings must have shown on my face, for Testa grinned and said, "I will give you a minute to recover."

"Not necessary. I am well aware of my physical shortcomings."

"Very well. For obvious reasons, I cannot divulge details of your assignment or of the techniques you will employ. Suffice it to say that you will be free to leave at any time, although if you do, you will, of course, forfeit the balance of your salary and living expenses. I also can reassure you that the risk will be negligible. Moreover, you will be on duty only one day out of two. The balance of the time you will be free to enjoy yourself and see Italy. You are already aware that the pay is quite generous."

I was indeed. While he talked I weighed various considerations. It might be many years before I would have the opportunity to see Italy. What did I really have to lose? I suspected that my missions would at least be harmless *at first*, while I acquired experience, and that any danger would appear, if at all, only late in the summer. If I were given an assignment I could not handle, I could simply refuse and return home. Furthermore I had read that homicide was uncommon in Italy, unless one provoked a Mafia chieftain. If I had only the equivalent of a free week, I could still consider myself fortunate and the object of envy. Moreover, there was little to keep me in the United States over the summer. Certainly, my stunted social life did not. I was lucky to get one date a month and never the same woman twice.

Signor Testa had paused, obviously awaiting my reply. I did not keep him waiting long.

"I accept."

"I hoped you would. Congratulations and welcome! When can you leave?"

"I am ready now!"

Actually, getting a passport and making travel and other arrangements required two weeks, during which time I received a letter announcing my appointment as a "consultant" to the Ministry of Tourism. My term was to begin at once and expire on the first of September. As promised, my airline tickets and other expenses, up to a reasonable limit, were met by the Ministry of Tourism.

I arrived in Rome in early June and was summoned at once to the Ministry for several days of orientation, provided by a Signor Tucci. He was very unlike Testa in appearance, being short, rotund, and florid, but he shared with the latter a penetrating stare and a lively sense of humor. This was apparent at the onset.

"Try to assume a naive and foolish expression. Perfect!" However, I had changed nothing, being too startled to react.

"No offense. I couldn't resist. You are very patient with us, Signor Mosby. That is important too, of course."

He then got down to business. My first assignment concerned the swarms of vagrant children who were tormenting tourists in Rome and elsewhere. Some were Gypsies, some came from Calabria or Apulia, but most were refugees from the Balkans, especially Albania and Bosnia, as well as a few from elsewhere in Eastern Europe. Their *modus operandi* could not be simpler. A half-dozen or more would silently surround a usually solitary tourist and then jump him all at once. Three or four would grab his arms, immobilizing them. A second group would seize his wallet or even rip open his shirt and snatch his money belt. Any money would be quickly removed and dispersed among the group. They would flee in all directions. Whatever had contained the money would be discarded.

"The important thing to remember," said Tucci, "is that they work very fast. Typically, it is all over in thirty seconds. Sometimes they work in silence. Sometimes they scream their heads off."

"How old are they, typically?"

"While they can be any age, they are most commonly eleven to fourteen and usually female. This protects them from the more violent forms of physical battery. Middle-class tourists do not like to strike children, especially girls."

"What do you want me to do exactly?"

"I was coming to that. You will stake out a high-risk area, dressed in casual but expensive clothes that we will provide, and carry a wallet stuffed with marked bogus money. The wallet will be large enough to make a significant bulge in your pocket. It is important that you seem to be isolated. You should avoid being close to any group. Also, it would be advantageous to appear preoccupied, as, for example, being immersed in a guidebook. Finally, you will be equipped with this."

He produced a miniature spray can and beckoned me to follow him into a well-ventilated second room, where a white cloth was hung from the ceiling. Motioning to me to stand well back, he held the can at arm's length and discharged it briefly at the cloth. I had expected some kind of mace or pepper spray, but instead a very bright red stain appeared on the cloth. But this was not all. There was also a powerful stench, like ten thousand grilled Limburger cheese sandwiches.

I stepped outside the room hastily. Tucci followed me and closed the door. When he spoke, it was with a grin. "While the stench will fade away after a few hours, the color will last for days without special treatment. Ordinary soap and water are ineffective. The stink is detectable a block away. The color confirms the identification, as do the marked bills."

"What happens then? Are they arraigned and tried?"

"Not as a rule, unless they have done something serious, such as battery resulting in severe injury. We prefer to handle the matter administratively. We simply ship them back to their country of origin. It is quite unusual for them to possess the appropriate immigration documents."

After a pause, he resumed: "Are you ready to start?"

"Yes, of course."

"Tomorrow you will begin at the Spanish Steps. You will walk by casually, continue until out of sight, and then return after twenty minutes or so. You must, of course, avoid seeming to patrol the area. I can almost guarantee that you will attract active interest. It is important to appear solitary and not part of any group. Naturally, you must also avoid showing too much interest in the people you encounter. Just act like any tourist. I suggest again that you have a guidebook and appear to be consulting it from time to time. The more preoccupied you look, the better.

"Leave your passport at the hotel. If—I should say *when*—you are accosted, do not attempt to fight back or apprehend them yourself—just use your spray. Be careful to wait until they are at least ten feet away. Keep the safety catch engaged until you are ready to use it. Aim for the lower halves of their bodies. You will probably not lose the wallet—they usually discard it a few steps away. If you do, don't worry; we will replace it. Your clothes have been chemically treated to minimize contamination by the spray. If you should get some on you, spray the affected areas with this. It will neutralize both color and smell."

He handed me a second can that had a white color and a tube of colorless ointment that I was to rub onto exposed skin before beginning my rounds.

"Actually, there is no reason to contaminate yourself. The can produces a thin jet of liquid about twenty feet long. Just wait until they are well away from you before spraying. I am sure it is unnecessary to stress that it is better to let them go free than to risk spraying an innocent passerby."

Finally, he asked if I needed directions to the Spanish Steps. I did not. I had intended to visit the famous landmark anyway. They were within easy walking distance of my hotel. Tucci handed me a carton containing the clothes I was to wear. I had supplied them with measurements while still in America.

The next morning I donned my new expensive yet informal international-style clothes. They did not suit me. I looked more foolish than ever. I sighed and set out for the Spanish Steps. I had been told to expect a very mixed crowd and this indeed proved to be the case. Soldiers, government clerks, and tourists of all nations were mingled, as well as some nondescript stationary individuals who seemed to have no particular occupation. However, I saw no young people. I walked past the steps, as I had been instructed, sauntered on a few blocks, and returned after a decent interval. I repeated this several times without incident.

However, on the fourth pass, I found myself involuntarily enveloped in a dense crowd that pressed tightly against me. Upon placing my hand in my pocket to check my wallet, I found there was already a hand in my pocket. I grabbed it by the wrist, but it pulled loose with a sudden jerk. Its owner disappeared into the crowd. I got a brief glimpse of the back of a male with long, disheveled hair. As the sidewalk was too crowded to give me a clear line of fire, I could not use my spray. While I drew a few curious stares, the incident did not arouse much interest, as if it were a routine occurrence.

I had not scored, but neither had I lost anything, so I could consider the episode a draw. Henceforth I would avoid crowded portions of the sidewalk, and if I found others approaching too close, I would withdraw to the periphery next to a wall and come to a dead halt. However, this proved unnecessary. The crowd had thinned somewhat and I had adequate spacing.

I approached the limits of my beat and paused before turning back. I became bored and almost decided to dismiss the whole project as a boondoggle. Thus my guard was down, and I was poorly prepared for what happened next. Except for one detail, it fit Tucci's description perfectly. My first signal that an attack was imminent was a loud scream that came from a girl about thirteen years old. She stood about three feet in front of me. I froze momentarily and felt my arms seized by two pairs of female hands, while two other hands entered both my pockets. About six young girls had converged on me from nowhere, screaming and yelling as loudly as they could. I learned later that they were yelling, "Let go of her! Leave her alone!"

As Tucci had predicted, it was all over very soon, and the girls scattered in different directions, leaving the now-empty wallet at my feet. My arms were now free, and I was able to retrieve my spray can, which I aimed at the back of the nearest girl. However, I had forgotten to flip the safety latch, so nothing happened when I pressed the release button, although pressure obviously built up inside.

Cursing inwardly, I released the safety latch, although all the girls were now out of range. A jet of liquid shot from the now randomly aimed can and was intercepted by an elegantly dressed middle-aged woman. She was instantly converted into a scarlet and evil-smelling apparition. She now began yelling in Italian at the top of her lungs, easily exceeding the girls in sound volume. Although I had learned a little Italian, the only word I caught was *pazzo*. I offered her the decontamination spray can, but she shrank away from me.

A small crowd had begun to gather when a policeman appeared. He could speak English, and I did my best to explain the situation, showing him my ID from the Tourism Ministry. He was apparently familiar with our project, for he did not seem surprised and only shook his head resignedly. He spoke to the woman in Italian and finally persuaded her to let him spray her with the decontaminator. The odor vanished, and her exposed skin was bleached, but her clothes were ruined. The policeman took my name and number and let me go.

When I got back to the hotel, there was already a call awaiting me from Signor Tucci, requesting my presence urgently at a conference. Signor Tucci and two other men, who I had not seen before, were awaiting me. Tucci's smile and patronizing manner were both gone. He came at once to the point:

"Signor Mosby, this is a most unpromising beginning. Not only have you failed to catch anyone, but we are left with a five-hundred-dollar bill for the lady's clothes. There were those who felt you should be shipped back to America without delay, but more lenient views prevailed." The other two men looked at me grimly. It was not hard to guess who my detractors were.

He continued:

"I'm sure it is unnecessary to remind you again that you should arm your weapon before you use it. You should not use it unless you have a clear line of fire to your target and to no one else." He continued for some time, giving me a number of practical hints, as well as a portable phone with which I was to report the time and location of each incident, as well as the number and description of my assailants. Finally, he told me that my beat for the next day would be the area around the Trevi fountain in the morning and between the Roman Forum and the Column of Trajan in the afternoon.

As I left, I passed a man who I recognized from the waiting room of the Ministry office back in America. We nodded to each other, but I did not feel like talking. I wondered if he would replace me at the Spanish Steps.

On the following day I exchanged my costume for one more conservative and wore a cap. My patrol around the Trevi fountain drew a blank. Once I had the feeling I was being watched and did indeed glimpse a nondescript man looking at me intently, but he at once averted his glance and walked away. It was a very hot day, and by noon I was exhausted and drenched in sweat. After a cold drink at a sidewalk cafe, I took a cab to the vicinity of the Roman Forum. Although the distance was not great, the ride seemed to go on forever, and the bill was preposterous. I paid, but resolved to pass the driver's name and license number on to the Ministry.

My first two hours at my new location were as uneventful as those spent at the Trevi fountain. From time to time I would see parties of several dozen tourists being led by their guides through the Colosseum, the Arch of Constantine, or the remnants of the Forum itself. Out of boredom I listened to several of the English-speaking guides' expositions. They struck me as sound but dull. I was careful to stand well away from the body of tourists as I had been instructed.

Finally, there was a lag during which two groups of tourists were within the Colosseum and the others had moved on. It was during this period when I was relatively isolated that I first felt a sense of menace for which there seemed no justification. The only people near me were a trio of two boys and a girl in their mid-teens, who seemed innocuous enough. I tensed as they passed me, but nothing happened; the girl gave me a pleasant smile. Two other teenage boys, walking independently, now overtook me and passed to my right and left. Meanwhile, the first trio had slowed, so that they were only a yard ahead of me. I glanced behind to see a pair of girls closing on me fast. I realized that I was now surrounded.

I happened to be near a discarded wooden box and sat down on it. They had not expected this, and there was a finite interval before they rushed on me silently. I capitalized on this to remove my armed spray can from the paper bag in which I had concealed it and to set my wallet, from which I had removed all the real money, on the sidewalk beside me. They were now more confused than ever and probably beginning to be suspicious.

However, one of the boys gingerly picked up the wallet, removed the marked bills in a swift motion, and threw the wallet back in my lap. This was followed by their abrupt departure and, shortly thereafter by a blast from my spray can. This time I was right on target and nailed all six, evoking a storm of shrieks and curses. One of the boys stopped and started to approach me. He looked very cross, and I wondered if he had a knife. However, just then a party of German tourists began leaving the Colosseum a few yards behind me, and the boy resumed his flight, leaving a lingering stench.

Several of the Germans had witnessed the fleeing and brightly colored teenagers, and their curiosity was aroused. However, their English was imperfect, and I spoke no German, so they soon shrugged and departed. Meanwhile I duly reported the incident and returned to my beat, changing my location to the area around the Column of Trajan. Nothing further happened that afternoon. I had ample time to study the Column with its reliefs showing the execution of Dacian prisoners. I dislike soldier-politicians and Trajan has never been among my favorites, but one cannot deny that he was one of the big winners of antiquity. What would he have been today? A stock market manipulator? A big time athlete? A general?

My portable phone did not ring, but there was a call from Tucci after I returned to my hotel. He was elated.

"Congratulations! You have redeemed yourself handsomely! We have captured all six, and they are on their way out of Italy. Moreover, we had two other hits today, for a grand total of seventeen. At this rate, Rome should be completely safe for tourists by the end of the summer." He went on for some time and then concluded by telling me that my next post would be the area around the Villa Borghese in the morning and the Pantheon in the afternoon. This time I drew a blank at both sites.

This set the pattern for the balance of my stay in Rome until the very last week. Tucci was careful to assign me to widely separated locales on successive days and encouraged me to travel out of Rome on my days off. Also, I suspended my activities for the day after each hit. On the average I scored a hit on about one day out of three or four, the frequency falling off later in the summer. Only once did I nail a group of more than six; two or three were more typical. There were no more serious accidents, although once I got a small amount of spray on my wrist;

I was easily able to neutralize it. Since I never had the same beat twice, I was able to familiarize myself with a large section of the city.

From time to time I recognized other decoys, some of whom I had met and others who I identified from their general appearance. Occasionally one of the latter would wink at me conspiratorially. I began to suspect that I was acquiring a reputation, since once or twice a group seemed to be converging on me and then veered off at the last minute. This was made more plausible by the appearance in early August of a short article in an English-language paper on the decoy program. Tucci was apparently successful in keeping the program out of the media, except for this lapse, which was not repeated.

I devoted my off-duty days to seeing as much of Italy as I could, being careful to make myself inconspicuous and to travel with organized groups. Nothing happened to change my opinion that Italy is among the most pleasant, civilized, and good-hearted nations on earth, as well as perhaps the most rewarding to the traveler. I had only one disappointment in that my social life did not improve. My efforts to strike up an acquaintance with the English-speaking girls I met at the hotel and elsewhere proved unrewarding, often drawing the suppressed smile I knew so well. Since I dislike commercial sex, I gritted my teeth and resigned myself to a celibate summer. Oh well.

On my last full day, I was assigned the Castel Sant' Angelo neighborhood in the morning and the Baths of Caracalla in the afternoon. The morning was typical. I walked around the Castel Sant' Angelo several times, as well as within it, and extended my patrol to the surrounding streets, always with my guidebook visible, while I pretended to consult it studiously. Nothing. Once I thought I saw three swarthy teenagers eyeing me furtively, but it was a false alarm; they split up and departed in different directions.

The afternoon was a different story. As it happened, there were not many tourists about, and I had the Baths largely to myself. As a result, I had a sense of danger, which had been absent in the morning, and I kept my armed spray can handy in its paper bag. Perhaps the oppressive spirit of the bloodstained and infamous emperor Caracalla affected my nerves.

Nothing happened for two hours. I began to feel bored again and looked at my watch when I felt myself seized by a stranglehold from behind. The grip was very strong, obviously not that of a young teenager. Two other men in their twenties emerged from behind the remnants of an ancient wall. One of them grabbed my empty wallet. I had forgotten to stuff it with marked bills. The other two tore open my shirt and felt around for a money belt. Finding nothing, they unceremoniously threw me to the ground, although I had made no resistance, and the largest gave me a vicious kick in the ribs. My paper bag had been snatched away, and my spray can lay beside me on the ground. Apparently, they had not realized its significance.

I was slightly stunned and they were almost out of range before I used my spray. Even so, to my regret, I missed the one who had kicked me. However, I managed to spray the other two to a moderate extent. This had the gratifying result of making them stop and curse in a strange language, and the alarming result of making two of them turn and head in my direction. Fortunately the third continued to run away.

It did not seem wise to take on odds, especially since they were individually stronger than I, so I began running toward the street. I moved very fast, for my heart was in it. Once again, salvation came from factors outside my control. Several soldiers happened to be passing by, and I succeeded in drawing their attention. My spotted and evil-smelling pursuers did not inspire confidence. The soldiers assumed correctly that I was the person in jeopardy and took my side. The two muggers could not adapt to the reversal in odds and withdrew. One of them made an obscene gesture.

The soldiers were at first inclined to be suspicious, but one of them knew a little English and, after seeing my documents, accepted my version. I duly reported the episode to Tucci and returned to my hotel as I had been instructed to do after each hit. I was summoned to his office the following morning.

This time Tucci was even more excited than on the previous day. "You have really hit the jackpot this time. Those men belonged to the worst gang in Rome. They are Russians—the stranded residue of a drug-smuggling group we broke up. They are cut off from their suppliers, cannot go home, and are desperate. The two you decorated led us straight to their lair, and we caught them, as well as a half-dozen others.

"In this case, there is no question of simply shipping them out, as they are suspected in several serious felonies in Italy, including at least two homicides, which are rare here. However, at least a dozen members are still at large, and as long as they are loose you are in serious jeopardy, for they are highly vindictive. I think it is time you left Rome. Quite apart from the Russians, you are beginning to acquire some local recognition, as you may have noticed.

"You have more than justified the trouble and expense you have caused us, and I would not blame you if you simply resigned at this point and either went home or treated the balance of your stay as a vacation. Since there are only two weeks left and we owe you some free time, I would not object to continuing your salary and per diem if you choose the latter. However, I must insist on your leaving Rome at once in either case."

I did not have to think long before announcing my decision. I had become bored with the work, and it was time for me to get ready for graduate school. I informed Tucci that I felt it was time to return home. The earliest date he could get me plane tickets for New York was two days later.

"I recommend strongly that you avoid walking on the street and take a taxi at all times. You will find that the hotel has changed your room. Do not answer the phone or admit anyone. Wear ordinary clothes, like the ones you flew in with. Whenever possible, I suggest that you have meals sent to your room. Incidentally, the decoy program has been a huge success. We have shipped several hundred young people back to the Balkans and elsewhere. Attacks upon tourists have almost ceased. However, I doubt if we will try it again. Our secrecy is blown and we want no tragedies."

I was somewhat disappointed. I still had not really seen all of Rome and now I never would. But I held my tongue.

Everything happened as Tucci had said. I took a taxi back to the hotel and found that all my belongings had indeed been transferred to another room, where I holed up for the night. I was informed with a smile by the waiter bringing the meals to my room that they were "compliments of the house" and that there would be no charge. I had no visitors, and although the phone rang once, I did not answer it, as instructed.

At breakfast the next morning, I requested and received an English-language newspaper. I opened it and froze. There on the front page was a photograph of Sam Karplus, one of our group of decoys who I had met casually in Tucci's office. As I read the story, the roof of my mouth became dry.

Karplus had been the victim of a brutal assault, which is very uncommon in Italy. He had apparently been abducted, savagely beaten, sprayed with his own scarlet dye, and dumped in a gutter. He had been hospitalized in serious condition. When asked for a working hypothesis, the police inspector had only shrugged and said, "Ivan was here."

Karplus had an unusually close resemblance to me. Side-by-side one could easily tell us apart, but when separated, we could readily be confused. Probably they would believe that they had disposed of the one whom they sought and abandon their search. Or so I hoped.

I spent the day reading in my room and was thoroughly bored by nightfall. It was my last night in Rome, and I thought I would take a chance and eat at a

first-class restaurant. I would dine early and return by taxi while it was still daylight.

However, while my afternoon had not been very strenuous, I felt tired and lay
down for a brief nap. I was awakened two hours later by the phone ringing. I
answered it automatically, forgetting Tucci's warning. An anonymous accented
voice asked, "Signor Mosby?"

"Yes."

That was all. Whoever was at the other end hung up. I did not have time to
think about this, for it was getting late and already starting to become dark.
Although the restaurant, which featured northern Italian cuisine, was only a few
blocks from my hotel, I took a taxi, requesting to be picked up in two hours. I ate
without incident. Service was slow, and it was almost midnight when I finished.
No cab was in sight and the streets were deserted. It had been cloudy all day, and
now a light rain fell, and a light fog rolled in.

I didn't like it, but there seemed no choice but to walk back to my hotel. After
all, I had told no one where I was going, and it was only a ten-minute walk to the
hotel. I had drunk almost a whole carafe of Chianti. I am not a frequent wine
drinker so I felt the effects of the alcohol. Perhaps it was this, together with the
poor visibility, that caused me to become lost.

In any event, I had been walking along in a somewhat muddled state and musing on the events of the past three months when I suddenly realized that I didn't
know where I was. There was no one around to ask for directions. I thought I
would retrace my steps to the restaurant and start over, but after walking for what
seemed like a long time, I could not see a single familiar landmark. The upscale
neighborhood of the restaurant had been replaced by one that was nondescript
and rather shabby. I must have headed in the wrong direction from the onset.

I decided it was time to stop and consult the condensed map I carried in my
billfold. It was at this time that I heard footsteps coming from the direction I had
just traveled. My first thought was that here was a possible source of assistance.
But as the source of the footsteps drew closer, I did not like what I saw. He
walked very fast, and I obviously commanded his attention. I thought of running
ahead toward a lighted area in the distance. However, two more figures now
appeared from nowhere, one across the street and the other about a half-block
ahead of me. All three converged on me.

I was now cold sober and thinking clearly. They were powerfully built men
who I was no match for; neither could I hope to outrun them. As they drew
closer, I thought I recognized one of my Baths of Caracalla friends. In retrospect,
I suspect that they may have been awaiting me along my logical route to the hotel

and only later extended their scan. I backed against a wall and tried to prepare myself.

When the nearest of them spoke, it was in accented English: "Good evening, turd. What a pleasant surprise!"

I knew better than to try to kick him in the groin; he would be expecting that. Instead, I went for his kneecap. It worked. He uttered an unintelligible curse and dropped his arms. I tried to hit him in the Adam's apple, but missed. All three were now upon me.

I have no very clear remembrance of what happened next, except that I took many blows and then kicks after I had dropped to the ground. Then there was a shout, then more, then many more. My assailants fled, and I found myself surrounded by solicitous faces looking at me anxiously from above. I heard expressions of shock and concern. Friendly hands got me into some kind of vehicle and unloaded me at some kind of emergency room.

Faces drifted into my vision and then faded out again—physicians, police, and unknowns—separated by periods of darkness. The last of these was the brutal face of Caracalla, who regarded me coldly with his blankly malevolent stare. I sensed rather than heard him tell me that I would never be the same again and that it served me fucking well right. After that there was a long period of oblivion.

After I came to, I learned that, considering the violence of the assault, I had come off surprisingly lightly. I had suffered a broken rib, a fractured jaw with the loss of some side teeth, a smashed cheekbone, and a broken nose. The damage, while significant, was not serious enough to require prolonged hospitalization, and I opted to return to the United States at once with my face in a kind of cast. I did not worry much about my appearance, which left little scope for deterioration.

Back in America, the day finally came when the cast and bandages were removed, and I examined myself in a mirror. I was first surprised, then puzzled, and finally gratified. My features had been rearranged to only a limited extent, but the change in overall impression, while subtle, had been quite significant.

I was still ugly, but I no longer looked stupid. My face was now asymmetric and somewhat concave on the left side. This, plus a bent nose and a loss of weight, gave me a somewhat gaunt and brooding expression, especially when viewed in profile from the left. No longer did I give an impression of foolish vulnerability. If anything, I looked feral and Byronic.

I decided against any form of plastic surgery to restore my original appearance, although my mother (but not my father) vehemently favored this course. I have modified my face only to the extent of letting my hair grow longer and adding

sideburns to conceal a nasty scar. On balance, my Italian adventure was beneficial. I have noticed that people are more inclined to take me seriously and my
social life has become far more rewarding, perhaps assisted by a form of romantic
cachet I have acquired. So, if my mother doesn't like my new identity, she will
have to lump it, for I have no intention of changing.

The Russians? According to Tucci, I was their last victim, if indeed it was
them. In any event, nothing more was heard of them. I could afford to forgive
them; they had done me a favor.

The Hiker's Tale:
At Anton's Restaurant

It was mid-February in an unusually mild winter, and there was no visible snow anywhere, although a sub-freezing temperature and slate-gray sky went with a forecast of light snow that night. Having arranged to be dropped off by the Chesapeake & Ohio towpath at Point of Rocks, well above Washington DC, my plan was to hike the fifteen miles south to White's Ferry. I had left my car there and would drive to my father-in-law's house in Bethesda, joining my wife and several relatives for dinner.

In my sixties, I normally walk a little less than three miles per hour. Thus, if I began the hike at 11:00 AM., I could expect to arrive at White's Ferry no later than 5:00 PM, leaving ample time to arrive for dinner at 7:00. I allowed extra time, because I was not quite recovered from a serious episode of influenza.

When I had arrived at Point of Rocks, my wife driving, we heard an updated weather forecast. The snowfall would now begin in the early evening. It would be moderate rather than light. I did not like the sound of that. As a pilot, I had learned that a change in predicted weather from mild to severe always occurred in stages. Moreover, the sky, while still gray, seemed to have lowered and darkened and to have a more blurred and diffuse texture. I had no way of knowing that I was observing the prelude to one of the worst blizzards of the century.

"Do you still want to go?" asked Ethel, my wife. "I don't like the look of the sky and you've been sick. Are you sure you feel up to it?"

I felt trapped by the planning and anticipation, plus the hour-long drive to Point of Rocks. As usual in such cases, I rationalized. It was only fifteen miles. This was not the Yukon, but only rural Maryland; I would never be more than five miles from a town. I had hiked through snow before. So my answer was yes to both questions. I got out of the car, kissed my wife good-bye, and began walking south on the towpath.

The town of Point of Rocks is best known for its train station, a gem of late nineteenth-century architecture on a still-working line. Clearly visible from the towpath, it is built of red brick and boasts a purely ornamental tower and cupola. Though of no practical value, this lifts the spirits of the viewer and rescues the town from anonymity. Point of Rocks itself contains a gentrified eastern section filling with tract houses and emulating the dreary developments spreading relentlessly through central Maryland.

The ungentrified western portion, which bordered my point of entry to the towpath, consisted of somewhat dilapidated older houses. Several of the yards displayed abandoned and rusting automobiles in addition to nondescript piles of other junk. Occasionally there were sounds of a violent argument proceeding within, sometimes in English, sometimes in Spanish. On this day I saw only one other soul—a fierce-looking older woman who regarded me from her porch with intense curiosity. I waved at her and walked on, crossing a wooden bridge over the old canal bed before stepping onto the path.

The first two or three miles of the path south of Point of Rocks parallel the old B&O railroad tracks, which are separated from it by the dry canal bed. On the other side the path is separated from the Potomac River by a secondary growth of mostly hardwood forest, through which the river is clearly visible. In mid-autumn the path is littered with the insipid, custard-like fruit of the pawpaw tree.

A mile south of the town, the occasional squatters' shacks found farther north had disappeared, and the only signs of human activity were the rails, the path, and the dried-up canal. About three miles south, the railroad diverged, leaving only the path and canal. The temperature had been below freezing for several days and the few pools of stagnant water in the canal bed were frozen solid. Through the trees I could see that a layer of ice covered the Potomac, except for a yellow-green channel in its center. At this point, I felt the first snowflakes.

The first snowfall of winter brings exhilaration. For the first half-hour, the snow was sparse, and I could enjoy the gradual transformation of my bleak surroundings. The wind had almost ceased, and I did not feel the cold too much, although I regretted not having dressed more warmly and especially not having worn something to cover my ears.

I now heard behind me the sound of a four-wheel drive vehicle heading south. Without looking, it had to be the solitary ranger who patrolled sporadically the upper towpath, to Cumberland. He was a thin, taciturn man in his mid-twenties, with a blond mustache. I had seen him several times but had never spoken to him. However, on this occasion he stopped his jeep and asked me if I knew they'd revised the forecast for up to two feet by morning.

"How much farther are you going?"he asked.

"Not much farther,"I lied. "Only about a mile or so."

He had the authority to order me off the trail and even to arrest me if circumstances warranted. But he only shrugged and drove on, the jeep's tracks showing clearly.

As I continued south, the intensity of the snowfall kept increasing. By the time I reached the Monocacy aqueduct, which is about seven miles from Point of Rocks and almost halfway to my destination, the visibility had been reduced to two hundred yards. About four inches of snow lay on the ground. Normally I would have paused at the aqueduct, which is a fascinating reddish sandstone structure that once carried the canal over the Monocacy River. It was now 2:00 PM I had covered seven miles in three hours, somewhat slower than my normal rate, but if I did not slow down, I figured I should reach White's Ferry by six, which would allow me to arrive for dinner by seven, as scheduled.

The snow, however, was now deep enough to make walking more difficult. A gravel road intersected the trail just past the Monocacy. I considered briefly whether it might not be better to go this way. It was about three miles to Dickerson, but then what? I should have to knock on some stranger's door and ask him to drive me to White's Ferry in what by now was a howling blizzard. I could not contact my wife by phone; she had planned to spend the afternoon at her parents' house, helping them prepare dinner, and I had not memorized their unlisted number. Continuing the walk on the trail seemed the lesser evil.

As I started on, I noticed a large black crow sitting on a wooden post, regarding me intently.

"Get out of this, you fool, while you can," said the crow.

But it was only a crow, so I nodded politely and went on. The next landmark was Pepco, the power-generating plant that supplied electric power to greater Washington. It was about four miles ahead. The intervening space was mostly occupied by farms. In summer I would have seen grazing cattle and sheep. Now the swarm of snowflakes was so thick that several times I stumbled off the trail and had to grope my way back.

I soldiered on, though I began to feel very cold and very hungry. Several times it seemed to me that someone was following at a distance just out of eyesight. Once I paused and waited for several minutes, but no one appeared. I passed a nearly buried milepost. Upon scraping the snow away, I learned that I was two miles from the Monocacy and six miles from White's Ferry. The Pepco plant would be about two miles ahead. But the shocking news was conveyed by my watch, which told me that the time was now three-thirty. It had taken me an hour and a half to cover two miles.

Even if my rate of movement slowed no further, I could not expect to reach White's Ferry much before 8:00, much too late to arrive at dinner at a reasonable hour—if I arrived at all. The snow was at least a foot deep now and walking in it was like trying to wade through a viscous liquid. Every step required a perceptible effort, and I had difficulty seeing the trail. Plus, my clothing was inadequate for a blizzard. I was starting to feel very tired. Seeing a fallen tree a few yards from the towpath, I sat down on the trunk to rest for a moment, although I knew well that this was unwise.

Soon, however, I noticed a sign just off the edge of the trail that I had some-how overlooked before. Its design was simple but in elegant taste, and it read: *"Anton's, the Best Restaurant in the World. 1/4 mile."*

In close proximity to the sign was a short bridge over the canal bed that led to a path lined on each side by a row of trees of a kind I did not recognize. Although they were, of course, leafless, their intermeshing branches provided enough screening so that the depth of snow was much less than on the towpath. Never mind the absurd presumption of the sign, all that counted now was to get out of the blizzard and into a warm place as soon as possible. I did not wonder why any restaurant, best in the world or not, would be accessed from a hiking trail with sparse traffic and set in the middle of nowhere. Neither did I consider that the restaurant might well be only open seasonally and, if so, would probably be closed in winter.

It seemed as if I had barely set foot on the path before I found myself standing before an upscale building with a sign discreetly identifying it as Anton's Restaurant. It was brightly lit and obviously open for business. A uniformed doorman opened the door for me, and another staff member helped me out of my jacket and hung it in a cloakroom.

I was in a kind of lobby with a huge fireplace in which several large logs were blazing. Down a short passageway, the main dining room was crowded with elegantly dressed men and women despite the early hour and forbidding external conditions. I could also see waiters dressed in tuxedos and carrying trays. It was clear that I had somehow stumbled upon an establishment *de grand luxe*. Normally I would have been embarrassed to be dressed in my nondescript hiking costume, but all other feelings were submerged in my gratitude for being out of the cold and in the warm.

As I paused on the threshold of the corridor, a tall man approached. His authority was conveyed by a rather military bearing and the unmistakable expression of one accustomed to being obeyed. He had a quintessential continental and Mittel-European flavor, somewhat resembling the late actor Anton Walbrook. His speech was formal and courtly, which seemed inappropriate for a bedraggled intruder like me.

"How many are in your party, sir?" he asked.

"Only myself."

"Then perhaps you would prefer the Gentlemen's Lounge?"

"That would be fine."

"If you would be so kind as to follow me."

He led the way into a wood-paneled room of opulent and mellow appearance with a fireplace of its own. A few well-dressed men were seated at separate tables. One of them was served by a waiter, who was, like the head-waiter, of refined and aristocratic appearance, although older, with white hair and a face registering sardonic humor. He reminded me somewhat of Claude Rains in his later years.

I now remembered my predicament and explained my situation to the head-waiter, who did not seem surprised. Was there any possibility of obtaining transportation to Bethesda? He regarded me with a look of mingled benevolent concern and pity, with a dash of amusement.

"But of course, sir. Do not give it a second thought. Your limousine transportation will be ready when required. Meanwhile, I hope we can prevail upon you to partake of our hospitality."

My failure to appear at the family dinner would cause considerable consternation, but it would now be rude to refuse; besides, my hunger was difficult to ignore. I was duly seated at a table. The waiter approached with a wry smile that made him look even more like Claude Rains and asked if I would prefer the complete or the short menu.

I took the short menu.

"And would you like to see the wine list?"

Why not? None of the entries on the list was familiar to me, and no prices were cited. On encountering unpriced items in foreign restaurants, I had always avoided them after the initial experience, which was unpleasant and expensive. In the present case I asked the waiter if he could give me some idea of the price range.

"Oh, for you there is no charge, sir. We are aware that you are an involuntary guest, and we would not dream of capitalizing upon your misfortune."

One could not beat that. Not wanting to seem too shameless, I ordered a bottle of domestic Chardonnay from California. The waiter brought the wine and placed the bottle in an ice bucket. While I sipped the first glass, he reappeared with the short menu that looked rather lengthy to me. The complete menu must have been of encyclopedic dimensions. Upon opening it, I found a bewildering melange of continental and regional dishes. As in the case of the wine list, all items were unpriced.

The soup section filled two pages. After considering shrimp soup with coconut milk, lemon grass, chiles, and tomato, and corn chowder with crab, Tangier style, I settled on Senegalese peanut soup, which I'd had before at an African restaurant at the 1964 World's Fair and liked. The salad section was even longer, occupying almost three pages. I selected hearts of palm and avocado, with raspberry vinegar.

The list of main courses was about a third of an inch thick. I did not know where to start and opened the menu at random, leading me to the section on game dishes. I hesitated long over the wild boar, but finally settled on venison with gooseberries, Alsatian style. The waiter took my order, bowed slightly, and left.

Wanting to keep some track of time, I consulted my watch. To my consternation the time was now half past seven. What had happened to the last three hours? I did not have time to consider this for very long before the waiter reappeared with the Senegalese peanut soup, the spicy aroma of which commanded my full attention. As I dipped my spoon into it with intense anticipation, everything vanished.

I was lying in bed in a room with pale green walls. A doctor and a nurse stood by the bed. My feet ached badly, and I felt very weak. It was several moments before anyone noticed that I was awake.

"You are very lucky indeed," said the doctor. He was a Pakistani with a British accent. "There wasn't much to spare."

I lapsed into unconsciousness before I could press him for details. Later, I learned the rest of the story from Ethel.

"Were you worried?"

"You better believe I was worried."

"Someone must have rescued me. How did it happen?"

"You owe your life to the park ranger. He became worried and commandeered a snowmobile to search the trail south of Point of Rocks. He found you lying beside a stump, half-buried in snow. He found you just in time. Your body temperature was about eighty-five degrees when you entered the hospital. It was miraculous that you got off as lightly as you did. I'm never going to let you go off like that by yourself in bad weather again."

I lost no more than one toe from my left foot and two from my right. I did not tell her that while my body was slumped beside the stump, my spirit prepared to feast at Anton's Restaurant

I was humiliated to learn that I had been found only about a half-mile south of the Monocacy. Somehow I had gotten turned around in the blizzard and had been heading in the wrong direction, retracing my steps; the wind must have been strong enough to obliterate my tracks, or else I was too groggy to notice details.

But the greater part of me survived to hike again. The missing toes were not a serious handicap. I have often walked along the same route, but always in good weather. Needless to say, I never again found the sign pointing the way to Anton's Restaurant. However I did meet the crow again, sitting on a post as before. He had nothing to say this time but simply gave me a scornful look and flew away.

Although, upon reflection, I suspect that Anton's limousine would have conveyed me to a very different destination from Bethesda, I have always regretted that I was not allowed to get further into my meal. While hearts of palm salad often figures in our meals at home, I have searched in vain for Senegalese peanut soup and venison with gooseberries a l'Alsace. Perhaps in my final reverie I may return to my unfinished business at Anton's Restaurant, where a friendly welcome doubtless awaits me.

The Student Pilot

It was a late Saturday afternoon in early May. I sat nervously in the deserted office of Airways Flying Service, not knowing what to expect. I could only fall back upon the known, which was that someone had purchased a block of flying lessons at short notice. As I was the only instructor with available time, he had been assigned to me.

Another factor was that he was an Italian whose English was imperfect, and I was the only instructor who knew any Italian at all, although I was quite rusty by now. Since nothing hinders instruction like faulty communication, I wondered if I had bitten off more than I could chew. I instructed only on weekends; the rest of the week I spent working as a technician at a government laboratory. I speculated that the reason this job had fallen to me was that no one else had wanted it. An unusual aspect was that the student was not seeking a license, which seemed to make little sense. It was not a good sign.

Although I heard no one approach, I was suddenly aware that I was not alone. Two men regarded me silently, neither of whom I had seen before. One of them, whose appearance I could never remember afterward, addressed me:

"Mr. Robert Malkus?"

"Yes."

"Allow me to present Carlo Malatesta, your student pilot. I have made arrangements on his behalf."

The other man now stepped forward. I extended my arm to shake hands, but instead he bowed slightly. I was so struck by his appearance that it was a moment before I spoke.

"Buon giorno."

"Good afternoon."

He was a man of about forty, with dark blond hair and beard. In appearance he was tall and muscular, as well as unusually handsome, beautiful in fact. I was also surprised to find that he spoke perfect, although slightly accented, English. Either I had been misinformed, or he was an uncommonly fast learner.

"Is it correct that you are not seeking a pilot's license?"

"That is so."

"Do you have a logbook to keep a record of your training?"

"That is unnecessary. I wish only to learn."

"Have you ever flown before?"

"No."

Stranger and stranger. He must be some kind of rich eccentric, I thought, or perhaps he is simply crazy. My bafflement must have shown on my face, for he gave me an ironical smile. I looked around for his companion, but he had vanished. I felt obligated to start the lesson, despite my substantial and growing misgivings. Before we began, I made my usual short speech, of which the most relevant part was:

"Ninety-five percent of the time, flying is almost as difficult as riding a bicycle. It is the remaining five percent that your training is designed to deal with."

He smiled silently and nodded, as if to signify appreciation of the sentiment.

We walked to the plane, a Cessna 152, attracting many curious glances from other pilots. I did the conventional walk-around, pointing to and naming the primary components of the airframe. I drew his attention to the cross-sectional shape of the wing, with its curved upper and flattened lower surfaces. I started to explain how the pressure differential arising from this shape as the wing passed through the air generated lift. I noticed that he didn't seem to be listening but was lost in thought. Then he smiled and held up his hand.

"*Basta.* I think I understand."

This was the first time I had heard him speak a word of Italian.

He continued. "The air has farther to travel on the upper surface than on the lower and it must do so in the same time, so its velocity is greater, hence an upward force. It is the same principle as tacking a sailboat."

I had to think for a moment as the idea was new to me, but then I realized he was basically correct. I turned next to the propeller and pointed out the curved shape of its surface. He did not comment this time, but he obviously understood that it was another case of the same principle. Next I showed him the engine. This seemed to be new to him, which puzzled me, and he asked many questions, which I did my best to answer, with indifferent success. Although he did not appear to be altogether satisfied with my description, it was time to start the actual flying, as the sun was sinking below the horizon.

We entered the cabin, into which he fitted with difficulty. He grasped without being told what the seat belts were for and fastened them. I started the engine and pointed out the different flight instruments and explained their functions. In each case he nodded his head after a moment, signifying that he understood perfectly what was going on. Only in the case of the artificial horizon did he question me further.

I taxied to the active runway and took off. The air was so smooth it was hard to pinpoint the moment when the wheels left the runway. A change now came over my companion. Whereas before he had seemed happy but relaxed, he now assumed a look of joy and savage exultation. I demonstrated the use of rudder and aileron in banking and turning and the elevators in climbing and descending.

"May I?" he asked.

I nodded, not without misgivings, and released the controls to him. He proceeded to execute several simple maneuvers, which he performed flawlessly. In particular, his coordination was close to perfect, which is unusual for any student pilot and, for a novice, unheard of. I thought either he was lying about his lack of experience or he had natural talent of a very high order indeed.

I proceeded to demonstrate maneuvers of increasing difficulty, including steep turns, slow flight, and stalls. To my continued amazement, he was able to carry out each of these perfectly on the first try with faultless coordination, neither slipping nor skidding. If he was indeed a beginner, he was certainly the best student pilot I ever had and in a class by himself. Then, in a perverse moment, I proceeded to demonstrate recovery from a spin. This was manifestly unfair and would have scared the wits out of most novices, but his only visible reaction was a momentary look of puzzlement. Then, to my further astonishment, he asked:

"May I do that too?"

"All right, but climb up to six thousand feet first."

I was ready to take over at any moment, but this proved unnecessary. His spin entry and recovery were perfect, probably better than mine.

It started to get dark, so we returned to the airport, where I demonstrated a landing, which he observed somewhat impatiently. I then told him to take off, fly around the traffic pattern, and land. I was no longer surprised to find that he performed both operations smoothly. As we taxied back to the tie-down, I noticed that, while his exultation had calmed somewhat, he still seemed possessed by intense joy.

"May I schedule again?"

"Yes, of course. Same time next week?"

He nodded in acquiescence. I noticed that his original companion had reappeared and was waiting by the office. I turned to the plane for a moment to lock the cabin door, and when I turned back again, both men were gone.

The following week was a busy one at work, which drew my thoughts away from Malatesta most of the time. However, whenever my mind was free, they returned to him in bewilderment. What was going on? Was he on the level, or was this some kind of scam? But what possible motive could he have for wanting to deceive me? I had no money to speak of, and any cash flow would be in the wrong direction from his point of view.

My aggravated curiosity would give me no peace until I called the manager of my small flying school and asked what he knew about my new student. The answer was short and to the point.

"Nothing at all. He appeared out of nowhere. He, or rather his colleague, paid in cash, which is unusual. Is there a problem?"

"Not really. He seems to be an unusually fast learner. It's hard to believe he's never flown before. Is it possible to do a background check on him?"

"I suppose so, but it's a lot of trouble, and I hate to start without good reason. You're thinking he might be an illegal immigrant?"

"Doesn't seem like the type, but maybe I'll ask to see his visa next time." However, I forgot this.

During the following week, I had many preoccupations and had half forgotten my peculiar student when the arrival of Saturday jolted me into remembrance. The weather had changed much for the worse. A cold front had swept through, removing the low clouds and haze that had predominated during the middle of the week, but bringing strong winds and turbulence. Had it been an ordinary student, I would have been tempted to cancel the lesson, but I felt a strong curiosity to see how Malatesta would react to adverse conditions and exposure to the other side of flying.

Most novice pilots begin with enthusiasm, which can last a long time. But sooner or later there is a bad experience, a real or imagined peril. The way in which they react to this experience determines whether or not they go on with it. Most do not.

My student and his companion appeared abruptly at the scheduled time. As before, I did not see him approach. This time his escort did not speak but simply nodded slightly and departed.

I thought it only fair to warn him about the changed conditions.

"The flying will be very rough today because of the wind. We may be knocked around a bit. Do you still want to go up?"

"Of course," he said with a puzzled expression.

I shrugged, and we walked in silence to the plane. This time he assumed command of the plane at the onset without asking and took off. I opened my mouth to protest this usurpation of my prerogatives but closed it again as I realized that he was perfectly at ease in these conditions. For an hour we repeated all the standard maneuvers. The turbulence was worse than I had expected, and even an experienced pilot might have had difficulty in controlling the plane. But Malatesta took it in stride and indeed seemed to be enjoying himself more than ever.

Finally it was time to land, and now I was really worried, for the wind had shifted, and we had a sixty-degree crosswind at twenty knots. Even under stable conditions, it would have been a severe challenge to keep the plane moving straight down the runway by a sideslip. I thought it was time to take over.

"You had better let me handle the landing. A crosswind landing under turbulent conditions requires practice."

"But there is no problem. One uses the ailerons to start a turn into the wind and opposite rudder to stop actual turning."

"Very well, but I'll take over if you get in trouble."

He laughed at this. There was no trouble. His crosswind landing was as flawless as his other maneuvers. In particular, he had no difficulty adapting his side slip to a wind that varied continuously in both velocity and direction.

Afterward I asked, "Do you want to schedule again?"

"I'm afraid that will be impossible. My time is up, and I will have to go back."

"To Italy?"

He did not answer but smiled a little sadly.

"There is not much more you can learn from me. You are obviously a born pilot."

This time he consented to walk with me back to the office. Because he had not used all the time he had purchased and was entitled to a refund, there was still some minor paperwork to be completed, although his companion was obviously impatient.

A wall of the office was covered with posters and photographs illustrating the history of aviation, which drew Malatesta's attention at once. They were arranged in the order of their historical periods, the most recent being on the extreme right. The latter depicted the space shuttle and the big military and commercial jets of our own day.

Then there was a sequence displaying some of the famous fighter planes and bombers of the World War II era, preceded by propeller-driven planes of the '30s. Still earlier, there was a photograph of the *Spirit of St. Louis,* with its pilot standing beside it. He lingered long over this. Then there were fabric-covered planes of the World War I period. Next were the early prototypes of the Wrights and Santos-Dumont and, still earlier, the gliders of Lilienthal.

But the display did not end here. Following a very wide gap of time, we found ourselves in the 16th century. We saw what looked somewhat like a very old version of a fabric-covered aircraft but without an engine. Malatesta's face showed first intense interest, then recognition, and then wild hilarity. He spoke very rapidly in Italian to his companion, driving his fist into his open hand.

The other had withdrawn a little and spoke to me in subdued tones. It was the first time I had heard him speak on this day.

"You see, he woke up early, while his contemporaries still slumbered."

It was not much to go on, but suddenly I understood everything.

"Then, his name's not Malatesta, is it? His real name is—."

But he only smiled silently while he tugged at the other's arm. At this moment I was distracted by a sound I heard outside and turned my head away for a moment. Looking out the window, I observed at a short distance the most beautiful woman I had ever seen. I have had no trouble in remembering her face, which wore an archaic half-smile. All this could not have required more than a few seconds, but when I turned back, both men were gone, this time for good. When I looked out the window again, the woman was gone as well.

CANINE FANTASIES

We walked briskly through the fog and drizzle so characteristic of November in our part of the Midwest. We were late, and Elaine was moving as fast as she could and urging me on to greater efforts. I did not want to arrive at all, but it was some time before my reluctance surfaced.

"This is the silliest yet," I said. "Even if he's on the level, what is the point? What do you expect to learn?"

"I have no expectations at all," said Elaine, "except that it will be an interesting experience."

"I'm sure," I said.

From then on we walked in silence. Finally, we arrived. The meeting place was a room in a suburban senior center that had been engaged for that purpose by the local seniors group; however, the meeting was open to all. About thirty people were there. Most of them seemed of middle age or younger and must have been outsiders like we were.

The speaker, Dr. Calfano, was not an impressive-looking man. He was short, fat, and balding. He was said to be a medium and a clairvoyant, as well as a hypnotist. However, the program for this evening was solely hypnosis, slanted toward entertainment rather than therapy. I was only vaguely familiar with hypnosis and was unsure of how much substance it might have.

I took no stock at all in his other alleged specialties. If he indeed practiced them, it would tend to quench any slight interest I might have in his hypnosis. Elaine had reservations about the former, but assured me that hypnosis, about which she had done some reading, was a very real phenomenon. I wondered idly whether it was necessary to be a true believer in order to be a suitable subject.

At about ten minutes after the announced starting time, when it had become apparent that no more audience was coming, Dr. Calfano began his lecture. I now noticed that, despite his rather humdrum overall appearance, he did have one exceptional feature—his eyes. They were very dark blue and set deep in his skull, giving him a very penetrating gaze, which made me uneasy when it was directed toward me. I felt that I had seen such eyes and such a piercing stare somewhere before, but I scrolled through my memory in vain. Perhaps he reminded me of a picture of Rasputin.

The talk began on a rather low-key note with a historical introduction to hypnosis. Dr. Calfano went out of his way to disabuse his audience of some popular misconceptions about the subject. In particular, no one in the hypnotized state could be made to do anything that he or she would be unwilling to do when awake. It would, for example, be impossible to seduce an unwilling girl by the use of hypnosis. The same was true of post-hypnotic suggestions. The general tone of the talk was conservative and scholarly, rather reminiscent of a sober lecture in a university classroom. I began to suspect that I had misjudged Calfano; perhaps he was not the charlatan I had expected.

Nevertheless, the fact remained that I was not profoundly interested in the subject, and I was glad when he brought his lecture to a close and began the demonstrations, first calling for volunteers. There was not an overwhelming response, but several hands were raised, including, to my alarm, Elaine's. However, he did not choose her but picked instead a younger woman who looked like a college student. The process of hypnosis, which took much longer than I expected, consisted of monotonous assurances that she was getting sleepy, while she viewed what seemed to be a complex and highly mobile optical pattern displayed on a screen. When she finally succumbed, Calfano proceeded to transport her back to specific times in her childhood, including her eighth birthday, and to elicit accounts from her about what happened. She spoke in childish tones appropriate to her putative age. There were no lurid revelations; indeed, it was all very ordinary and rather dull.

The next volunteer was a middle-aged man with a tough and pugnacious face. He proved to be resistant; Calfano finally gave up after about ten minutes. He had no better luck with the third volunteer, a placid woman of about forty. The audience was now becoming distinctly restive, and several slipped quietly away. When he called for his fourth volunteer, I raised my hand, partly out of sheer boredom and partly to forestall Elaine, who I was afraid would be receptive and say something silly. I thought that if he failed with me, I would be in a strong position to suggest that we leave and go home.

Calfano accepted me as his next subject. It was an easy choice since I had no competition. I came forward and sat in the armchair set aside for this purpose. He began his churning optical display on the screen. I simultaneously heard his voice insisting that I was weary and sleepy. Actually, I did not need to learn this from him, as boredom and the lack of activity had already made me drowsy.

The demonstration abruptly ceased. Calfano, now wearing a smile, thanked me and indicated that my part in the proceedings was over. I thought that he had given up rather easily in my case and that surely Elaine would be willing to leave now. However, as I got up to return to my seat, I noticed that the audience, including Elaine, regarded me with amused interest. I looked at my watch and was amazed to find that half an hour had elapsed since I had arisen to go to the demonstration armchair.

This was far too long to be accounted for by the brief period I recalled. So it appeared that he had not failed with me after all. I had not been an especially willing subject, but I had been too bored and apathetic to put up much resistance.

It was getting late and Calfano now brought the meeting to a close. The audience applauded and a small group remained behind to question him further. Clearly I had saved the day for him. As we walked out, I felt wide awake and very curious as to what had gone on during my period of unconsciousness, especially since Elaine kept smiling at me archly. As soon as we were alone, I asked her what had happened and especially what I had said.

"Nothing bad happened," she said. "And you didn't say anything indiscreet. It was like it was with the first woman, except you were more articulate than she. He took you back to your childhood. You remembered your father and talked about him." This did not surprise me. I remembered my father even in my normal conscious state, although he had died when I was only five.

"You also talked about a dog you had when you were ten. I think his name was Scout."

This gave me a profound shock, for I had completely forgotten about Scout and had not thought of him for more than twenty years. Now a good deal came back in a rush. We had been very close, for I was an only child without many friends and my mother had withdrawn to a private world where she could be alone with her grief.

I scrolled compulsively through my memory, which bore me like a current to the implacable conclusion. Scout had been struck and killed by a speeding car while retrieving a rubber ball I had thrown too far. The driver had not even slowed down. I had been very sad for a long time and had never gotten another dog.

I said nothing of this to Elaine, but she must have sensed from my silence and altered countenance that she had awakened a painful memory and was silent herself until we arrived home, although several times she seemed on the point of speaking. Not only was the memory traumatic, but I could not seem to shake it off. My thoughts remained gloomy until a new distraction slowly claimed my attention. This first took the form of a generalized uneasiness that did not assume a concrete form until we were approaching our car, which was parked several blocks from the meeting place. I then felt a strong sensation of being followed, and followed closely, which did not arise from any obvious clues. Several times I found myself pausing and turning to look behind us. There was nothing to see but a deserted street and nothing to hear but our own footsteps.

The feeling did not vanish as we got in the car. If anything, it grew stronger. Indeed, after my third furtive glance at the back seat, Elaine suggested that my hypnosis had left me too nervous to drive and offered to switch places, but I rejected the idea and promised to keep my attention focused on the road. We arrived home and entered our front door. I had to make a conscious effort not to look behind me.

It was not till we were in the house that I seemed to hear something for the first time. It was not a sound in the ordinary sense; rather it was entirely inside my head, as when one mentally recalls a tune heard in the past. However, this was not a human sound, but rather somewhere between a yawn and a growl, as one might expect from a large and bored animal.

I heard nothing more for a time, but I was still conscious of an unseen presence, which made itself felt independently of the five senses. It was neither benign nor menacing, it was simply there. A sound similar to what I had detected earlier recurred shortly before I got into bed, but this time it was of much shorter duration. I had said nothing about all this to Elaine, but some of my inner stress must have shown, for her amused look had been replaced by one of guilty concern.

Surprisingly, I had no difficulty in falling into a deep and dream-free sleep, from which I awoke abruptly at 4:00. My thoughts returned to the unknown presence, which was still there although attenuated, and especially to the sounds. Although I had heard no more, I now realized what they had been. They were canine sounds, such as a large dog would make. However, being able to identify them was no great comfort; there were several possible explanations of their origin, all unpalatable. In particular, the idea of a brain tumor, of which my father had died, now arose like a malevolent apparition and refused to disappear. Then my thoughts reverted to the already half-forgotten hypnosis session, and I resolved to question Elaine more closely about what had happened.

For the remainder of the night I drifted in and out of a shallow sleep, from which I awoke little refreshed. Elaine was already up, and I launched my enquiry without ceremony:

"I want to know all that happened last night while I was out. Did he give me a post-hypnotic suggestion?"

Elaine nodded sheepishly. "Yes, but it was nothing bad. You were to think you were being followed by a large black dog for one week. He asked me not to tell you, but I made no promise. Have you been feeling anything?"

"I sure as hell have. Why did you let him do it?"

"It seemed harmless enough. Perhaps your telling him about the dog you had when you were a child gave him the idea. But surely the spell will be broken now that you know."

However, the illusion did not go away; indeed it became, if anything, stronger. My unseen companion did not leave my side as I walked to my car that morning and accompanied me as I drove to work. Finally, my sense of his presence became so powerful that I, quite irrationally, turned my head to look at the back seat. At this moment I heard a loud yelp inside my head, such as a dog might make when struck by a thrown stone. It was much stronger than anything I had heard the previous day. Abruptly, my external surroundings reclaimed my attention, with a screech of brakes to my right. Out of reflex, I braked hard, causing another screech of brakes from the car behind me. I had gone through a red light.

Less than a yard separated me from the car to my right, whose bushy-haired youngish driver glared silently at me. As I drove away I saw in my rearview mirror that he was giving me half of a V-for-Victory sign. Served me right. If I had had an accident, I could always have explained that I was distracted by a phantom dog.

That settled it. As soon as I arrived at my office, I called Elaine and told her to get Calfano's local address and phone number and to treat it as a matter of some urgency. She did not call me back at work, but the balance of the day passed without incident, although my unwelcome visitor never left my side. There were no more sounds, except that twice I thought I detected the same bored yawn I had felt the day before. As usual, at 5:00 I left my office carrying my briefcase, walked to the parking garage, and drove home. My apprehensions had subsided somewhat. I began to get used to my invisible canine.

I arrived at home to find that Elaine had drawn a blank. The friend from whom she had learned of the lecture warned that it was the last in Calfano's series and that he planned to return to Argentina that very day. Elaine had obtained from her the name of his hotel, but a call there revealed that he had already checked out.

There was nothing to do but wait and hope that the problem would indeed solve itself at the end of a week. No one knew Calfano's address in Argentina. He was not on the staff of any university or governmental department and apparently operated out of his home, wherever that was. Locating him would involve some trouble and expense and did not seem worth it.

However, nothing changed at the end of the week. The signals I received, whatever they were, grew neither stronger nor weaker. The only occurrence that made me at all uncomfortable was the low snarl I seemed to hear during an interview with my immediate supervisor, a hard-faced woman who I disliked and whose goodwill I doubted. I must have started visibly, for she paused and looked at me quizzically for a moment before continuing. But this was minor. I did not need a spectral dog to tell that she was not a friend.

On the tenth day, largely at Elaine's insistence, I made an appointment with a psychiatrist for the following day. I told him what had happened with as much precision as I could muster. He listened rather impatiently to my account of the hypnosis and the post-hypnotic suggestion but questioned me closely about my symptoms, asking the predictable questions about insomnia, headaches, dizziness, and fainting spells. Clearly, he did not like it. He scheduled me for a series of clinical tests designed to "rule out a physical cause," meaning, I suppose, a brain tumor.

Nevertheless, the tests, which required a week to complete, were uniformly negative, so he was forced to fall back upon a purely psychological explanation, citing as an off-the-cuff hypothesis that the hypnotic session had somehow triggered a latent pathological tendency. To prescribe a drug would be guesswork, since no known drug addressed my particular symptoms. In any event, I was not in any distress or discomfort.

He suggested, without much conviction, that I consult a psychoanalyst and provided me with a name. There was more, but it was just words. He was obviously now somewhat skeptical about the entire tale. As I rose to leave he bent over and pretended to pet an imaginary dog. I was not very amused.

The psychoanalysis would have been expensive and time-consuming, and I decided, upon reflection, not to pursue it. After all, I had as yet no very disagreeable manifestations to complain of.

As I drove home I attempted to analyze the exact nature of what I was experiencing. One detects the proximity of another human or animal by the signals of sight, hearing, smell, and feeling. The sensations produced by sound or smell may be so weak as to lie below the threshold of conscious awareness and still alert us to another presence. In addition we can respond to the small rise in temperature that another body can produce in an otherwise empty house. Perhaps the latter explains why, upon returning home, I always knew if Elaine was in the house, even if she was asleep in bed.

In the present case, while sight could be ruled out as a factor, the other modes of perception could not. I have already alluded to the occasional canine "sounds" that were too conspicuous to be overlooked by my conscious state. But a corporeal large dog does not need to vocalize to produce a medley of subtle sounds arising from his digestive processes, as well as the noises produced by his rubbing, scraping, and rolling interactions with his surroundings. These are difficult to interpret individually, even if one's attention is focused upon them, but collectively they help to tell us that the dog is present in a darkened room. The same may be said of smell. One may not be conscious of the faint musty smell of a healthy dog, but its absence is noticed.

Likewise, a slight rise in temperature might be detected without being recognized as such. Perhaps parallel effects were occurring in the present case, except that the sensations were produced, as well as detected, within my own mind.

Thus far, I had no idea what my dog looked like. Not only did I never detect even a fleeting glimpse by my ordinary waking vision, but there was no sign of any latent image formed in my brain. This was so even if I closed my eyes and focused my attention upon him, although I remained, as usual, very conscious of his presence. Nevertheless, if my waking self could not see him, my sleeping self could and did. Toward the end of the fourth week, I had an unusually vivid, although entirely benign, dream.

I seemed to be walking along a path in a dense forest of oak, maple, and tulip poplar trees. It was a day of brilliant sunlight, which had no trouble in filtering through the canopy of leaves overhead. I had the same sense of freedom and peace that my everyday self would have felt in a real sunlit forest. As an experienced dreamer, I knew I had nothing to fear. But on this occasion I was not alone. I realized, as one does in dreams, that my companion was my elusive canine presence.

A few paces ahead of me walked a very large black dog, I judged to be an Alsatian. He was all that a dog should be, with glossy fur, white teeth, and intelligent, pensive eyes. At one point, as I fell somewhat behind, he paused and turned his head toward me, with a look grave and majestic. It was a look neither friendly nor hostile, but rather one of disinterested concern, as if he were checking up on a responsibility he had assumed. One thing was for sure, it was a world-class dog of magnificent presence. Calfano had evoked only the best for me.

After this, I lost any residual feelings of apprehension or discomfort. What I had acquired did not seem to be a pet, but it was in no way hostile. However, Elaine was still worried and blamed herself. She had finally located Calfano's address in Argentina and, unknown to me, had written him a letter, to which she received no reply. Indeed, we were not destined to see or hear from Calfano again. Meanwhile, I had gotten used to my spectral dog and paid him no more heed than if he were an unobtrusive real dog. Elaine and I had an unspoken understanding that neither of us would ever again acknowledge the dog to another person and when the psychiatrist made a gratuitous telephone inquiry, she informed him, with my consent, that the dog was no longer a problem, which was true enough.

During this early period the dog generally remained unobtrusively in the background, although I always knew he was there. However, exceptions did occur, and I have already alluded to two of these. A third occurred in the third month. I had been detained at the office and left for home very late, asking Elaine to save some supper for me. It was after 10:00, and I had a walk of several blocks along a deserted street to my parking garage. Pending construction of a new office building in the suburbs, the headquarters of my company had been compelled to remain in the center of town, which, like inner cities everywhere, was beginning to slide downhill. Even on the short walk to the garage I passed several "For Sale or Rent" signs and at least one boarded-up store front.

However, I was indifferent to my surroundings, being still immersed in a work-related problem that I had been unable to solve. Suddenly, I was abruptly recalled from my reverie by a tumult within my head. I seemed to hear very loud admonitory barks, as from an aroused watchdog. I turned my head and saw that "we" were not alone on the street. A shabbily dressed man rapidly closed on me from behind. He was not especially large or strong, but he had the obsessive, desperate look of a longtime heroin user.

I do not know what would have happened if I had not been alerted to his presence. As it was, he at first came to a dead halt, as if uncertain what to do next. Then his look of uncertainty changed to one of fear, and he nodded and walked past me, turning off at the next side street. I wondered what he had seen in me that was so scary. Surely he had not heard the canine sounds my brain had called up. In any event, any potential harm had been diverted. Indeed, if anything the episode had been beneficial, freeing me from my gloomy introspection.

When I impulsively told Elaine about this incident, it made a deep impression on her, and she could not resist passing it on to her mother, a devout Catholic. The following evening I received an excited and confused phone call from the old lady, who raised the possibility that the dog might be some form of guardian angel. Alternatively, he might be an emissary of Satan, who was attempting to gain my confidence so that he could more readily divert me to his own dark purposes.

She urged me to accompany her to a priest she knew who was said to be an expert in exorcism. Although I had no better explanation to offer, the whole rational, logical, scientific side of me rebelled at the idea. I thanked her and declined as politely as I could, telling her that Elaine had greatly exaggerated.

I was very cross with Elaine afterward. "Don't do *that* again, for God's sake," I said. "People will think I'm mad as a March hare."

"How do you know they don't already?" she answered.

I had no apt reply. However, she told no one else, and I avoided the topic with her. This was easy to do, for nothing significant happened for several months. My life was quiet during this period, both at work and at home, and I had no dreams and heard no pseudo-sounds, except for an occasional yawn.

About four months later I was preparing to leave on a business flight to Chicago. It was seemingly a perfect day for flying, being cloudless, although very hot and humid, a condition shared by the Eastern and Midwestern states for the preceding week. I arrived at the airport to find that my flight had been delayed indefinitely because of mechanical difficulties, but that space had been found for me on another airline that proceeded to Chicago by an indirect route.

I had opened my mouth to consent, when, for the first time in months, I heard admonitory canine sounds. This time it was not barking but a mournful howl, like a wolf baying at the moon. It was so unexpected and compelling that it deprived me of my faculties for a few moments. When I recovered, I found myself clutching the counter while the ticket clerk stared at me. I muttered something, picked up my bag, and left. The clerk was still staring as I left the terminal. However, the howling ceased as abruptly as it began.

By driving nonstop at top legal speed all night, I was able to arrive at Chicago the next morning. My trip took me through a band of very intense thunderstorms in central Illinois. A rapidly moving cold front had passed through the Midwest the preceding day and had produced severe convective activity, including several tornadoes.

After checking in at my hotel, I bought a local newspaper from the drugstore attached to the lobby and scanned it eagerly while I ate breakfast. While the paper carried on the front page a story about the storms and the damage they had caused, nothing was said about any airliner crashes. In particular, there was no mention of Delta flight 207, either in the paper or on TV.

So I had learned something new. There were limits to my dog's powers. He could reliably detect a current menace, but he could not infallibly predict the future. This was somehow reassuring, bringing him closer to me. Also, it made him less likely to be a Satanic agent, unless of course the destruction of the plane was contingent upon my being in it. This was getting out of hand. I had to pull myself together. As if in confirmation, I seemed to hear a low growl, such as a real dog might employ to discourage an irritating presence. I resolved to say nothing to Elaine, and she is unaware to this day that I drove to Chicago.

I did not know it, but only about two years of normal life remained to me. They passed quietly and, by and large, happily. It is worth mentioning that, not long after my trip to Chicago, Elaine encountered an acquaintance who had been involved in organizing the original hypnosis meeting. The acquaintance had heard indirectly that Dr. Calfano had been killed in a train accident in Italy, but had been unable to confirm it. In any event his current whereabouts were unknown. It was unlikely he could take the spell off now. I did not care.

During this uneventful period, there was only one instance when my dog was obliged to come to my rescue. This occurred during a business trip to Sao Paulo. I had left my hotel for an early morning walk before breakfast. Rather unwisely, I had departed from the broad boulevard on which the hotel fronted and strolled down a narrow side street. I passed a group of bored-looking youths who appeared to be about twelve to fifteen years old. Teenage males of no particular occupation are a fact of life in Brazil, and I paid them no attention until the well-remembered canine tumult went off in my head.

Seeing no menace in front, I looked back in time to see a bicycle quickly bearing down on me. If I had not dodged so that I received only a glancing blow, I would probably have been knocked to the ground. As it was, I remained upright, although shaken. I was immediately surrounded by the boys and felt solicitous hands all over my clothing, especially in the vicinity of my money belt. The pandemonium of barking did not cease until the boys suddenly withdrew their hands, as if they had touched something hot, and stepped back with scared looks. They then departed hastily, although they had no logical reason to do so, as I had made no hostile move. A hurried inventory showed that not only my money belt but also my wallet and passport, which I had foolishly carried with me, were intact. So once again my protector had done his job. But what had scared them? This was the second time it had happened. It was a question to which I still have no answer.

Nothing much happened after this until the final catastrophe. My life continued quiet and pleasant. I was somewhat apprehensive when our next-door neighbor acquired a Labrador retriever that was friendly and highly inquisitive. I had no trouble imagining all sorts of dismal scenarios, none of which materialized. Indeed there was absolutely no reaction, either on the Labrador's part or within me—not even a low growl. Apparently my own dog was beyond jealousy.

The catastrophe to which I have alluded did not come upon me entirely without warning. About a week before it occurred I had a curious prefatory dream, which was only the second, and thus far the last, in which I perceived a distinct canine image. However, the surroundings were vastly different this time. Instead of a sunlit forest, we were in a kind of parkland, with individual trees scattered in an endless sea of grass. It was very dark with no moon and no source of light except the stars, which were very bright and arranged in exotic and unfamiliar constellations.

There was a kind of path through the grass, along which we ran, this time side by side. In contrast to the first dream, I felt an acute sense of menace, as if we were being pursued by some poorly defined evil. The dog was as splendid-looking as before, but now when he turned his head in my direction I seemed to detect a look of consternation, as from one pressing against the limits of his powers.

I awoke abruptly and slept no more that night. While I could remember every detail of my first dream, this time my recollections were blurred and faded quickly. I felt that I had received some kind of warning, but of what? The next few days were very quiet and uneventful, and I was less conscious of the dog's presence than before, as if he had withdrawn a short distance. I did not know what to make of this, but was too preoccupied with other things to give it much attention.

My last day of ordinary life began like any other, except for a curiously heavy and oppressive feel of the atmosphere. It was late July, windless, and very hot and humid, as it had been all week. The sky was cloudless but had a blue-gray appearance, as if perceived through a layer of ground mist. The weather forecast had warned of an approaching cold front, with the likelihood of strong thunderstorms and a possibility of tornadoes. On my walk from the garage to my office, all I encountered was moist heat so severe that I felt as though I were wading through a warm viscous fluid. I was perspiring heavily by the time I gratefully reached the air-conditioned building.

The day passed uneventfully, but my dog was clearly restive, and I heard occasional low growls. I seemed to sense that he was in continual motion, first withdrawing a short distance and then returning. This is the way dogs act when they are trying to lead one somewhere. However, I was behind on my paper work and ignored the signals that might have saved me.

As the afternoon progressed, his restlessness seemed to increase. Finally the message became impossible to ignore. The growls changed to a prolonged whine and then to a high-pitched howl, which would retreat and then come back. I found that, if I walked in the direction of the elevator, the sound did not diminish, but that it became more shrill if I returned to my desk.

At last it dawned on me that the dog wanted me to take the elevator and leave the building. This was communicated with increasing urgency. Meanwhile, the sky outside had changed from blue-grey to an almost solid black. Only about a minute elapsed between the first raindrops splashing on the windowpanes and the onset of a deluge, accompanied by a high wind. The electricity now failed, plunging us into semi-darkness.

The canine din inside my head had now become overwhelming. It was not yet 5:00, but I decided to leave. Clearly, something was up. The elevator would of course have stopped, so I took the steps. As I walked to the landing, my wretched boss looked at her watch and glared at me.

The hell with her. Although I raced down the steps in double-quick time, my internal racket did not decrease but came now as a series of high-pitched despairing pulses, resembling shrieks. However, as I reached the front door, these were drowned out by a new and very loud sound—somewhere between a whine and a roar—coming from outside. As I opened the door and stepped outside, I was instantly soaked by a torrential downpour. What commanded my attention was not this, but what seemed to be an onrushing vertically-developed cloud, undergoing a violent internal churning. I did not know exactly what I was looking at and hence could not really see it clearly. However, I knew it was time to run for dear life and I did so, for my heart was in it.

I had gone only about a half block before my ordinary life came to an abrupt end. My only remembered sensation is of being hammered into the ground by a relentless pounding force. My unconscious state must have lasted a long time, during which I seemed to be trying to get to my feet and into some form of shelter, which I never found, unless darkness can be considered a shelter. The dog? Either he had withdrawn or I couldn't reach him.

When I awoke, it was into an almost totally dark world. I could just barely detect a difference between having my eyelids open and shut but could not differentiate objects from the faintly luminous blur into which they were merged. I was obviously in a bed rather than lying on the pavement.

"Is anyone there?" I called out. No one answered, but I was not alone. My dog was right there, and I'd never felt his presence more strongly. It did not seem judicious to try to get up, so I remained lying there, waiting for someone to come. My body seemed undamaged, but there was a bandage on my head. It seemed like a long time, but probably it was no more than five or ten minutes before I heard footsteps and then a female voice—a nurse? a doctor?—telling me that I had been hit by a flying object hurled by the tornado and that the damage was confined to my head. The voice also assured me that I would be all right, as I indeed proved to be, except for one detail. Later, when I seemed up to it, the voice told me that I had been lucky, that the street had been devastated, that my office building was a pile of junk.

I did not ask whether my boss had survived. I was done with her either way.

There is not much more to tell. My recovery was rapid up to a point. With time my vision improved to the point where I could not only tell light from dark but perceive Elaine as a prolate blur, which I learned to recognize. However, the improvement stopped there. I will never drive a car, watch television, or read an ordinary book again.

I offered Elaine her freedom, but she would not hear of it.

"From now on, I'll be nothing but a liability and a burden to you."

"I'm the best judge of that. If I should ever want to split, I'll let you know."

As it turned out, I exaggerated. While I cannot drive I can get about on foot perfectly well. In particular, I can walk several blocks to the store in perfect safety. You see, I have the most reliable canine guide a blind man ever had. When his yelp tells me it is safe to cross the street, I know that I can cross as confidently as if I were in my back yard. When, by another admonitory sound, he tells me to stop, I do so. With a complex set of signals, he guides me up and down steps and through crowded sidewalks. Once within a store, he directs me infallibly to the relevant counter. For a time I tried to use an elongated cane that Elaine had procured for me but soon found it redundant.

A well-meaning charity offered to provide me with a trained guide dog and was astonished when I refused and still more when Elaine refused to reason with me. I also learned later that my insurance company had become suspicious and had detailed an investigator to monitor me. Perhaps this was the reason they scheduled a non-standard follow-up examination to confirm my continuing disability. After this, I made a point of carrying the unnecessary cane again whenever I walked in public.

I am not quite finished. For a long time now I have ceased to regret what happened. It freed me from the routine of my dismal job and enabled me to undertake more rewarding work as a writer.

Moreover, I am not really blind. I was not surprised that my senses other than sight would be sharpened, but I had not expected that a form of sight would return. This requires that my eyelids be closed and owes nothing to my feeble residual vision. The images I perceive are entirely within my head and are somewhat like the mental pictures of sheep jumping over a fence that some invoke to promote sleep. However, they are much stronger, and I can choose them at will. With practice and concentration I can jump in an instant from a beach on Oahu to the roof of the Milan Cathedral or to the Taj Mahal.

I wonder if many blind people have this ability. It may be that in my case it was there all along, but the images were swamped by the everyday sights of my gritty Midwestern city. So in my case, at least, it seems to be true that when God shuts a door, he opens a window.

THE RETURNING STUDENT

I sighed and looked at my watch, which indicated ten minutes to six. I had overestimated the time required to drive to Urban University and now found myself with ten minutes to kill before my first lecture, a graduate-level course on chemical thermodynamics. I had no premonition that I was about to embark on the greatest adventure of my life.

To my surprise, there were already about a half-dozen students sitting in class. One or two were reading, one was dozing, and the rest were staring vacantly at the blackboard or at nothing at all. With two exceptions they were all black, in keeping with the overall composition of Urban University. Of the two exceptions, one was Chinese, while the other was a white man in early middle age.

It was the latter who drew my attention at once. Not only did he differ in age and race from the others, but also in his restless motions and the tormented look on his aristocratic face, with its high forehead and deep-set eyes. His general appearance was somewhat disheveled, including an untidy mustache and clothes that looked as if they had been slept in. They also seemed to be of an old-fashioned style, although at the time, in the early '70s, this was not an unknown affectation. His complexion was somewhat florid, like that of an alcoholic, and I wondered momentarily if he could be a street person who had wandered in to get out of the cold. However, the ironical smile he assumed when our eyes met tended to contradict this, as did a general impression of alertness. I had also a slight sense of *deja vu*, but this is commonplace for teachers, and in my case it is often triggered by nothing at all.

He had aroused my curiosity, and I would have spoken if I had not been distracted by a question from another student. By the time I had answered him, the lecture hall had filled with students and it was time to begin. From the podium I looked at a very heterogeneous collection of faces. While blacks of all hues predominated, there were also Arabs, Chinese, Latinos, Indians, and Iranians, as well as a sprinkling of whites, also quite mixed.

Urban University was a non-selective public institution, essentially open to all who could pay. In the sciences, its graduate courses were largely taught by moonlighting government workers like me. I had learned to expect a very wide distribution of abilities and interest. Some were as good as graduate students anywhere; others did not belong in any college. The one thing the members of my class had in common was age. With one exception they were all young.

This single exception continued to interest me. However, I did not arrive early for class again and had no further opportunity to speak to him alone. My next encounter with him did not come until the first exam, after I had finished grading the papers. I should explain that the distribution of grades in an exam at Urban University tended to be somewhat unusual. Instead of the usual bell-shaped curve, the distribution was bimodal, with only one of the modes being bell-shaped. The other had a maximum not far from 20 out of 100 and with the frequency of a zero grade being by no means negligible. I usually made my first test difficult, with the purpose of getting rid of the second mode early.

However, this time the distribution was trimodal. In addition to the usual two modes, there was a third mode, consisting of a sharp spike corresponding to a single individual and reflecting a perfect score. This had never happened before, and I double-checked the paper with great care but could not find a single flaw in it. A second anomaly was the smooth character of the old-fashioned handwriting. There was not a single erasure or correction.

The name on the exam book was "Auguste Dupin," and I reached for my grade book to give him a 100. However, the name did not occur in the grade book, nor in the class register, either among the regular students or the auditors. My curiosity was aroused, for it is not every day that one encounters such selflessness in a student at Urban University or anywhere else. Assuming no mistake had been made, here was a student willing to work very hard without hope of compensation. After I had handed back the other papers, I announced that I would like a word with Mr. Auguste Dupin after class.

I was not altogether surprised to find that Mr. Auguste Dupin was none other than the middle-aged white man who had attracted my attention the first day. When he introduced himself, I was somewhat puzzled by his ultra-refined Southern accent that one might have expected of a University of Virginia student several generations ago. He spoke slowly, with a somewhat old-fashioned locution and elaborate courtesy, most unusual anywhere today and especially so in a school for the masses like Urban University.

"Mr. Dupin, I can't seem to find your name on any class list anywhere, even as an auditor. I presume you are aware that, if you want to obtain any official recognition of your attendance, it will be necessary to register. If you register as an auditor, there will be no charge. Have you registered as a student for any course?"

He shook his head silently.

"Do you have a student ID?"

Again he shook his head, this time with a twinkle in his eye.

"I should warn you that it is against regulations to be present on the campus after hours without an ID. You could be forcibly removed by the security guards or even arrested."

"In principle, perhaps, but in practice it is unlikely."

"Do you have any reason *not* to register as an auditor? That way, there would at least be some permanent record of your performance. I cannot help being interested, for, judging from your first test, you are in a class by yourself. If you don't register, all memory of your outstanding achievement will be lost, as will the opportunity to obtain academic credit."

He displayed a gentle smile. "It doesn't matter. I am here only to learn for the sake of learning and have no practical application in mind."

I handed him his paper.

"Very well. However, if you have no objection, I will take the liberty of recording your grades in a special file so that they may be available if you should change your mind."

"As you wish. You are most kind."

And with that he took his leave. After he had walked out the door, it occurred to me that I should record his social security number, and I went after him. However, there was no sign of him, nor did he answer my call.

Officially, the man was, of course, a trespasser, and perhaps my duty was to report him. But he had done no one any harm, and it was gratifying to have at least one person of superior ability in my somewhat lackluster class. That his initial performance was no fluke was demonstrated on the second test, on which he again received a perfect score. This time I did not bother discussing it with him but simply handed it back with the rest.

During this time I noticed other idiosyncrasies of Dupin. He always sat by himself so that no one sat in the seats to his left and right. Usually he achieved this by sitting in the front row, which for some reason was always sparsely occupied. If someone else chanced to sit beside him, he would excuse himself and move to another seat. Moreover, he was always among the first to arrive, so that I never saw him come through the door. Also, he was always among the last to leave, waiting until the room was almost clear. It was as if he dreaded the possibility of close physical contact.

The following week I happened to be chatting idly with another chemist who worked at the same government lab as I and who also taught an evening class at Urban U. Our conversation turned to that institution, of which neither of us held an elevated opinion.

"You know, incredibly enough, I think I may have a genius in my class." He taught quantum mechanics.

"Is his name Dupin by any chance?"

"Yes, it is. I gather you have him too. He's very mysterious. He won't register and seems to have no plans to use what he learns. I suppose I'm not obligated to grade his exams, but I do so anyway, largely out of curiosity. I can't understand what a man of his age and ability is doing at Urban University. Do you think it's a question of money?"

"I don't know. Possibly. He may have decided to change fields late in life and can't afford a more prestigious school. Or perhaps he works during the day and needs a place with evening classes. I'd certainly like to help him if I can. Even at his age, he should have no trouble getting a scholarship or a student loan. I'll suggest it to him when I see him next."

"He's not an easy person to talk to. I've tried to question him about his goals, but all I get are evasions."

During the balance of the fall semester, I was preoccupied with unexpected problems of my own and quite forgot about Dupin. As expected, he again got a perfect score on the final exam. I made a Xerox copy of his final and filed it. I had meant to speak to him when I returned it, but a woman student distracted me at the last minute, and he retrieved the paper and left silently before I could turn to him.

During the winter break, which occupied most of January, there was a horrifying crime on the campus. A girl leaving the library in early evening was brutally raped and battered into a coma. As a result, campus security drastically tightened. Most entries to buildings were kept locked, and a guard was posted at all hours at each of the exceptions. Identification was demanded of everyone entering or leaving. There were also random checks of persons inside.

I feared for Dupin. He would never be able to slip casually inside without ID now. I was surprised therefore when I saw him sitting in class for the first lecture of my spring course, the topic of which was statistical mechanics. This class was much smaller, and I could make personal contact with students more easily than before. Out of curiosity I said, "You must have changed your mind about registering, since they let you inside."

But he only shook his head and smiled his quiet smile. However, I thought I detected an overtone of derision in his smile, which I had never noticed before.

A week or so later I drove off without my wallet, which contained my ID. When I tried to enter the building, the security guard refused to let me in, although he knew me by sight perfectly well. He was of course a complete imbecile, but he had his orders. I stalked off, thinking that if I drove home for my wallet, the round trip would require at least thirty minutes, and no one would wait that long. Just then I noticed that a normally locked door was now ajar and Dupin stood there beckoning to me. I entered, and he closed and locked the door.

"I can't thank you too much," I said. "I should have had to miss the class, and it would have been my own fault."

"Speak no more of it. These little *contretemps* occur in the best regulated lives."

He had saved my life, but I now began to wonder a little. He obviously was a man of parts; his talents not confined to academic matters. The ability to enter and leave a locked and guarded building at will is not usually cultivated by the non-criminal portion of the population nor is the need to exist incognito. Did this mean that Dupin was really some kind of crook? It is not necessary to look or talk like a crook to be one.

I rejected the idea almost at once. The man was too much of a gentleman and his interest in science too sincere to be compatible with this. Also, what could he possibly find worth stealing at Urban U., a chronically hard-up institution? But no matter how hard I tried to put it down, the newly aroused suspicion kept reviving insidiously and gave me no peace.

If Dupin sensed my suspicions, he did not show it externally, although he occasionally looked at me questioningly. I felt that if I attempted to query him directly, he would take offense, and I would see him no more. Then I had an inspiration. A friend of mine, Paul Schwarz, was a renowned expert in both computers and the analysis and classification of handwriting. He had developed improved procedures for identifying handwriting samples, even in the presence of efforts to disguise them. He also claimed to be able, in favorable cases, to analyze handwriting for personality traits. As he was a paid consultant for the FBI, he had access to their data files and, in particular, to their enormous collection of hand-writing samples from known criminals, which had been organized and classified according to the parameters utilized by his own system.

I still had a Xerox copy of Dupin's last exam. I gave it to Schwarz with a summary of my concerns, but without naming Dupin. He did not seem very interested but promised to try to fit it in. However, as I was leaving, I noticed he was studying the paper intently with a perplexed frown. He seemed on the point of asking me something but changed his mind.

Dupin's performance in the spring semester was as flawless as before. I deliberately scaled up the difficulty of the first test in an effort to find his limits. When I graded the papers, I thought at first that he had met his match at last. His solution of one problem, which I had obtained from an advanced textbook, seemed to be incorrect. However, he remained after class and soon convinced me that the problem was ambiguous and that his solution was as correct as my own.

All this time Dupin never missed, or was late for, a class. Whatever trick he used to get in seemed to work every time. It was during this period that I saw him outside the classroom for the first and only time. I had stayed late to talk to a student in difficulties and it was a half-hour after my usual quitting time before I finally left the classroom and walked outside. As usual at this hour, the campus was deserted, and I was mildly surprised to see two people standing beside the path that led to the street. One of them was Dupin. His companion was a girl, much younger than he, with a pretty but rather emaciated, face and dressed in clothes that, though it was too dark to see clearly, gave the impression of being somewhat old-fashioned.

Just then the full moon emerged from behind a cloud and Dupin's face was clearly visible. It was, of course, the same face I had seen in class dozens of times but, perhaps because I now saw it without competing impressions, it struck me very forcibly. At last I realized beyond all doubt where I had already seen the face. My consternation must have shown on my own face, for Dupin gave me an ironical smile, saying only, "Good evening, sir." His companion said nothing at all but simply looked at me with a bemused expression.

I mumbled something in reply and left precipitately, while trying to collect my thoughts, which were making no sense at all. Somehow I got to my car and drove home. The phone rang as soon as I opened the door. It was Paul Schwarz.

"I've been trying to reach you all evening. I could not find any correlation between your student's handwriting and that of any criminal in the data bank. So this search was negative, with a high level of confidence. You can relax on that score. But, acting on a hunch, I also looked for correlations with the writings of a set of historical personages, for which a data bank is also available. In this case I found a very strong correlation with a well-known writer and poet of the nineteenth century, whose name is a household word. Within the limits of confidence, the two are one and the same, which is of course impossible. So my methods seem to have failed in this case."

"I am curious to know who this person was."

He told me, and I was not surprised. I thanked him and hung up. My next act on arriving was to seek out an illustrated history of American civilization. When I found what I sought, I studied it for a while and then set down the book. There could be no doubt now. I felt that I had stumbled on something much too big for me.

Emma, my wife, is a psychiatrist and had been working late. It was at this moment that she returned home and walked into my den. She stopped abruptly upon seeing me.

"What is the matter? Did something happen? You look like you've seen a ghost."

"That's good, that's very good. You're very perceptive tonight."

While I had mentioned Dupin briefly before, it was only now that I gave her the complete account. She was skeptical, as I knew she would be. After a time the alarmed expression on her face faded and she was able to converse naturally.

"It's not unknown for someone with a lot of charisma to find it hard to stay dead. I wonder how many sightings there have been of Elvis Presley and Rudolph Valentino. Besides, what possible connection with science could he have?"

"Actually, quite a lot. He was two men, you know. One was all poetry and macabre daydreams. But the other was logical and deductive. He essentially invented the science fiction genre, and his detective stories are masterpieces of rational deduction. He liked to set up logical puzzles and unravel them. On one famous occasion, while working as a reporter, he unmasked a fraudulent 'robot' chess player, by showing that, unlike all known machines of the time, the motions of the 'robot' were not periodic. It was subsequently found to be human-operated.

"He also showed a sustained interest in technology including, especially, manned flight. I could go on and on, but I suspect that if he lived today, he would probably be a scientist and a very good one. This side of him was suppressed in life, and what could be more natural than his wanting to develop it in a subsequent existence?"

"Nevertheless, the fact remains that no one has ever materialized from the next world before. It's contrary to science and common sense both. It's much more likely that some charlatan is capitalizing on your gullibility."

"I don't think so. He's not the type, and he's obviously very serious about science. Also, he's never tried to persuade me that he had another identity or indeed tried to persuade me of anything. If he is a fraud, he is a completely disinterested fraud. There are, of course, other more plausible explanations besides reincarnation. He had no children, it's true, but perhaps his absentee father had another son we know nothing about, and this is a descendant of that son with a fortuitously similar genetic makeup. Quite apart from that, Schwarz is generally believed to be both conservative and highly reliable, and he has never found anything remotely comparable to this before."

I had an uneasy feeling that my lame alternative explanation was as hard to believe as the other.

"In my younger days," said Emma, "I was an avid reader of the stories myself, and I agree that they often show an aptitude for involved reasoning. I especially remember *The Goldbug*, which was about a buried treasure map. Incidentally, I suppose you've noticed that the name he has given is that of the main character in *Murders in the Rue Morgue*?"

"No, I hadn't, but you're right. In solving that case Dupin falls back on scientific principles. First of all, he frees his mind from preconceived prejudices. Then he considers only the strictly relevant and reliable information. Finally, he disregards all explanations that cannot possibly be true. No human being could have gained entry to the scene of the crime. Whatever did gain entry was enormously strong and capable of using a sharp-edged weapon. This leads him inevitably to the truth."

"You've definitely aroused my interest, and I hope you learn more. But I wouldn't tell anyone else about this."

"No, I may have rocks in my head, but it's not solid rock. I'll keep it under my hat for now."

The following day while at my regular job, my restless thoughts were interrupted by the phone. It was Schwarz.

"Would it embarrass you in any way if I pursued this? My curiosity is driving me mad."

"No, but you're on your own. What do you want to do?"

"For now, I would like to meet the guy and, if possible, get a photograph. If I drop in on your class this week, would you be willing to introduce me?"

I had misgivings, but gave a reserved consent.

"I suppose so, provided you get his permission before doing anything, including taking a photograph."

It was agreed that Schwarz would claim, with unconscious irony, that he was writing an article about returning students and wished to include Dupin as an outstanding example of these. The photograph would accompany the article.

Everything went wrong at the interview, which occurred at the end of class. Dupin seemed to see through our ruse. When Schwarz attempted to shake hands, Dupin simply smiled slightly and bowed, keeping his hands by his sides. He listened silently to Schwarz's proposition and then spoke very succinctly.

"Thank you very kindly. I am appreciative of the honor, but feel I must decline for reasons I prefer to keep to myself."

And with that he turned on his heel and walked out. As he did so, another student, who was leaving hastily, chanced to brush against him and staggered sideways with a yelp of pain. He sat down heavily and rubbed his shoulder.

"That guy felt like he was made of stone. There was no give to him at all. It was like running into a statue."

Dupin was gone now, and I knew better than to look for him outside. Meanwhile Schwarz was more frustrated than ever.

"His appearance matches his handwriting. Do you think I could photograph him at your next class, using a concealed camera?"

"Please don't. Somehow I think it would be a very poor idea."

That was the second to last time that I was to see Dupin. At the conclusion of the next class, he remained after class of his own accord and waited patiently until the last of the students who wished to talk to me had left. When we were alone, I initiated the conversation before he could speak.

"Does this mean anything to you?" I asked and quoted: "'The history of human knowledge has so uninterruptedly shown that to collateral, or incidental, or accidental events we are indebted for the most numerous and most valuable discoveries, that it has at length become necessary, in prospective view of improvement, to make not only large, but the largest, allowances for inventions that shall arise by chance, and quite out of the range of ordinary expectation.'"

When I paused, Dupin continued the passage, citing the next few lines before pausing: "'It is no longer philosophical to base upon what has been a vision of what is to be.'"

"Witness Alexander Fleming and penicillin, as well as lysozyme," I added.

"I never deluded myself that I could deceive a clever gentleman like yourself for long. But it doesn't matter. My time is up. They are calling us, and we shall have to go."

We? Then I remembered the consumptive-looking young woman I had seen him with.

"Was this a kind of *refrigerium* then?"

"You might say so, except that my permanent residence is not what you are thinking of. There is a special place for people like me, rather pleasant, in fact, except that we are denied the dimension of time, and things are rather static. Perhaps for this reason we are allowed periodic furloughs, which nearly everyone else uses for passive observation, while remaining silent and invisible. A material space, from which all others are rigorously excluded, must be set aside for me. This has practical inconveniences, as you will have observed. That is why I prefer evening hours, when things are less crowded and also why I relinquish my space as soon as I no longer need it. That is also why I chose an obscure institution rather than Harvard or Stanford, which would find it more difficult to accommodate my anomalous and irregular position.

"Incidentally, I shall never regret having done this, even though I can never use my new knowledge or take it further. I envy the living for all kinds of things, but I know something that you will never know—the overwhelming beauty and splendor of your science, which you grew up with and can never really appreciate, but which I can view with fresh eyes."

"Will you come again?"

"It is hard to be sure, but I will try. However, it will probably be centuries in your future, if at all. Incidentally, it is far from assured that there will be a future."

He cocked his head as if listening to something undetectable by me.

"They are becoming impatient. I must say *adieu* now."

And with that he bowed and departed. As he passed through the door, I thought that I glimpsed momentarily the young woman I had seen with him earlier, but I could have been wrong. A minute or so after he was gone, a female black student rushed into the room in a state of high excitement.

"There's a huge bird flapping around outside. It scares me."

"Don't worry about it. It won't hurt you and it'll go away soon."

When I was alone in the room, I noticed a small sheet of paper on my desk, which had escaped my attention before. A few lines had been written on it in Dupin's unmistakable handwriting:

> By a route obscure and lonely
> Haunted by ill angels only
> Where an Eidolon, named Night,

On a black throne reigns upright,
I have reached these lands but newly
From an ultimate dim Thule—
From a wild weird clime that lieth, sublime
Out of SPACE—out of TIME.

"What does it mean?" asked Emma later.

"I'm not sure. I think maybe he's talking about dreams, with the implication that all this was just a kind of dream for him."

"There was so much I wanted to ask him, like how he really died."

I felt a great sadness stealing over me, and we spoke no more of Dupin that night.

The Disappearance

"Does anyone know anything about the whereabouts of Mr. Laplace?" asked the captain, addressing the assembled passengers.

The passengers began to get restless. It was the second roll call, and the man had still not shown up. Worst of all, it was beginning to get dark. If he were still in the water after the sun went down, there could be little hope for him. In the daytime there is a kind of truce in the waters off the barrier reef, but at night the predators move in.

The party line, which is always spouted by resort PR, has it that sharks present little danger to human swimmers. Nevertheless, that very week the Australian papers had cited two fatal attacks—one off Western Australia, the other near Cairns, not far from our current location. However, it was not necessary to invoke this kind of explanation. He could simply have drowned, perhaps as a result of a muscle cramp or heart attack.

The problem was further compounded by the fact that he seemed to have been traveling alone and apparently no one but me had any idea what he looked like. All that was available was his name, which appeared on the roster as M. Laplace. It sounded French, but one could not be sure. All that seemed certain was that he had signed the roster upon boarding the excursion boat but had not signed again after completion of the tour. A head count indicated that the number of visible passengers, which, according to the roster, had been 105 at the beginning of the tour, was now 104. A crew member with a bullhorn blared out Laplace's name over the water, the surface of which was scanned by a dozen anxious eyes. Nothing. Meanwhile, the crew carried out a very thorough search of the boat, including the toilets. Again, nothing.

There was nothing for the captain to do but give the order to return to Cairns, with or without Mr. Laplace. The passengers, who had been a rather jocular group on the outward trip, were now quite subdued and pensive.

Everyone resented this development that gave a somber twist to what had been until now a thoroughly enjoyable day. Indeed it was almost a perfect day for a cruise from Cairns to the Great Barrier Reef. The sky was a cloudless azure, and the sea was as calm as the Pacific can ever be. Its deeper parts were cobalt, blending into turquoise toward the reef. The passengers were divided about equally between Europeans/Americans and Japanese and included about two dozen children. On the outward voyage everyone was in a good mood, and there was a continuous hum of lighthearted conversation.

Before reaching the reef, the boat made a preliminary stop at Green Island, which had a fine sandy beach and a kind of zoo. The star of the zoo was an enormous crocodile named Cassius that, despite his comatose appearance, was reputed to have a ferocious appetite. In an adjacent pen there was a second, smaller crocodile, which was missing about a third of its tail. It was explained to us that it was a female, originally intended to be a mate for Cassius, but he had instead thought she was on the menu.

I mention this because the man I later identified as being Mr. Laplace was still with us, as part of the onlookers at Cassius' pen. I had also seen him briefly while checking in at my hotel. Once seen, he was not easy to forget. He was tall and muscular, with greying hair and a genuinely majestic face, like that of a benign Roman emperor, on which an ironic smile alighted from time to time. He looked like the sort of man I would like to cultivate, and I tried to think of a conversational gambit with which I could approach him, but nothing came. I was further bemused by the fact that something about him activated a faint chord in my memory, as of someone with whom I'd had a fleeting contact but who had made a strong and enduring impression.

"Excuse me, sir," he said, as he turned to leave. His cultivated voice was also dimly familiar. Surely I had heard it before.

From Green Island the boat cruised leisurely to the floating platform that was its base at the reef. Here we were to spend the remainder of the day. Snorkels and scuba gear were available for rent to the more adventurous who wished to explore the submerged reef, with the proviso that they must remain within a roped-off zone about an acre in area. This was directly above the reef, so the water was never more than about ten feet deep.

Experience had shown that the more menacing underwater species never ventured here during the daylight hours. Beyond the ropes the water color changed rapidly from light turquoise to deep blue, as the depth increased sharply. One ventured here at one's own risk, as there was no patrol boat to warn of the approach of a fin cutting the water.

For the more timid and sedate, there was a small underwater boat with portholes through which the underwater terrain could be viewed in perfect safety. I chose this for my first foray into the water. We were not confined to the enclosed zone and could cruise leisurely along the perimeter of the reef, which, on a bright day, is a tumult of color, arising from both the stationary coral builders and the mobile swarms of small fish that darted about like multicolored confetti.

After the underwater trip, there was not much left to do except go snorkeling or scuba diving within the enclosed space. Because there was a long wait for the scuba equipment, which also required a short training period, I opted for snorkeling. As I left the scuba area, I noticed that my Green Island friend was in the process of completing his training. He later vanished underwater, and I saw him no more.

Meanwhile, I passed a pleasant two hours exploring the upper surface of the reef. The experience was marred only by occasional encounters with a swarm of hyperactive Japanese children who kept splashing water into my snorkel tube. The schools of colorful reef fish showed little fear of me and moved in synchrony, as if they had been trained. Occasionally, they would wheel and dash away in unison. I had always heard that this could signal the approach of some tyrant from the deep, but none ever appeared.

The sun began to sink toward the horizon, becoming redder, and the distribution of colors in the sea and reef was subtly altered. There was also a change in the demeanor of the fish, which seemed to become more nervous and suspicious and finally disappeared altogether. I did not have time to consider this for long when I heard a bullhorn summoning me back to the floating base. I saw to my surprise that I now had the reef almost to myself. Almost everyone else had already left the water.

Before returning to Cairns, everyone had to sign the register again and be checked off. When it became apparent that one man was missing, the captain held two roll calls. In the second one, each person passed from one end of the base to the other as his name was called. It made no difference; there were still only 104 passengers onboard. It was at this time I noticed that the man I had seen on Green Island, and later in scuba gear, was not among them. He stood out so prominently that he would be hard to miss even in a group and impossible to miss when each passenger walked separately across the base.

I requested and received a few words with the captain. He had a worried look and was, in fact, in deep trouble. I wasn't familiar with Australian practices, but in America he would have been in grave danger of losing his license and perhaps of attracting serious litigation. I told him of my theory as to the identity of Mr. Laplace and asked him if all the scuba gear had been returned. He answered impatiently, "Yes, of course. We've checked both the scuba and the snorkel equipment twice. Nothing is missing."

This meant that if the man had departed the platform, he had done so as a free swimmer, unencumbered by any breathing device. The captain then asked the assembled passengers if any of them had noticed a man resembling my description. No one had, including the captain. There was nothing more I could say, and he dismissed me with a sarcastic look.

This last finding was difficult for me to understand. Assuming that I was still in possession of my faculties, it could only be explained by the excessive preoccupation of the passengers with their own affairs. They were nearly all couples or family groups. I and the putative Laplace were almost the only solitary individuals.

The mystery was partially solved as we were approaching Cairns. A small curly-haired individual with a somewhat raffish appearance identified himself as Laplace and explained that he had signed the register twice, using different names, as a kind of practical joke.

"Throw the bugger overboard!" yelled an anonymous Australian voice. However more lenient views prevailed. Perhaps he was a spiritual kin of the legendary French taxi driver who ignored stop lights because he was a man, not a machine.

This solved the captain's problem but exacerbated mine. The others might think what they wished. I was still certain that I had seen the man on the boat and on Green Island, and he was certainly not on the boat now. If Laplace had indeed signed the register twice, then the number of people actually on the boat would agree with the number of valid names. Either my man had not signed in at all, or his signature had somehow been effaced.

It was not until I got back to my hotel room in Cairns and was lying awake in bed, after two hours of uneasy sleep, that I was able to identify the memory that Laplace had evoked. It dated from long before and far away, in a Sunday church service back in America some years earlier. Our regular pastor was confined to a hospital, and for several weeks his Sunday morning sermon was delivered by a series of substitutes. How they were found has never been clear to me. Most of these were not very memorable and what they said was soon forgotten.

However, the man who spoke on this particular Sunday was very different. His topic was the "last days," as described in Revelation, which deal with the period just prior to the Second Coming of Jesus. It was the first time I had heard Revelation used as a sermon text, and the members of our mainline Protestant church rarely considered or discussed it. In fact, our regular pastor seemed somewhat embarrassed by this book and responded to the occasional question with a somewhat curtailed answer, often commenting that the text was obscure.

This was by no means the case for our visiting preacher, who attacked the subject with gusto, with no concern for the ironic or amused glances the congregation exchanged. His sermon, which he delivered with substantial eloquence, centered on the small group of true believers who were to be snatched away to paradise during the process sometimes called the Rapture, leaving behind no trace. He enlarged on this topic for the better part of an hour, oblivious to the growing restlessness of his audience. As if to anticipate questions, he summarized the qualifications for those so chosen.

First of all, they must believe, literally and without reservations, in the Apostles' Creed, which implies unconditional belief in the divinity of Jesus and a life after death. They must also believe in the literal validity of the Bible as the word of God. Given these beliefs, a blameless life could be taken for granted. For the beliefs themselves, there was no room for any inner reservations. One either had the faith or one didn't.

At the conclusion of the service, as was the custom in our church, the preacher met in fellowship with any congregation members who wished to question or discuss the sermon with him further. The congregation was a very mature and civilized group and their questions were polite, even if the questioner was skeptical.

"Will those chosen be aware of it?"

"Yes, of course. The qualifications are perfectly clear."

"Do you think you are one of them?"

"I know I am."

"Will there be any warning that you are about to be snatched away?"

"I don't think 'warning' is the appropriate word, but I cannot expect any advance notice."

"Is it correct that you will simply seem to vanish, leaving no trace behind?"

"Yes, that is the case. Opinion differs as to whether such things as clothes and tooth fillings will remain."

"Will all the chosen disappear at once, or over a span of time?"

"I do not know. The numbers, of course, are minuscule, so it may be some time before people become aware of what has happened."

"Is it a one-way process, or can the chosen return at will?"

The speaker hesitated briefly and seemed to think before answering.

"I do not know. The scriptures are silent on this."

All through the interview, I was struck by the gap between the man's manner and appearance, which were urbane and cultivated, and what he was saying, which seemed to me to be the most amazing balderdash.

After about a quarter hour, my curiosity was not satisfied, but it was quenched. I left the group and walked slowly back to my car. I passed several small clusters of people who were heatedly discussing the sermon. As might be expected, their comments were almost entirely adverse and critical.

"What left field did this guy come from?"

"Whoever invited him?"

"He's just about 2000 years behind the times."

"Leave that sort of thing to the witnesses."

"But you have to admit he's an impressive man."

He was indeed, but the press of personal concerns soon drove him from my memory until the reef cruise awakened the latent memory. Could he be the same man? How could I be sure after the lapse of a dozen years? I could not, of course; in fact, it was wildly improbable. I strained to recall his name, but nothing came. All I could remember was that it contained the "ig"or "ix"sound. Higman? Bixly? Sigmund? I went through about two dozen of these before giving up.

Quite apart from this, how had he managed to disappear from the base? If he had simply swum away, it must have been without the aid of diving equipment, so he would have been confined to the surface. One of the lifeguards who continually scanned the area would surely have spotted him. Also, if Laplace was telling the truth, his signature must be somehow missing from the register.

I was inclined to reject out of hand the explanation that he was indeed a participant in the Rapture. But then where was he? Also, why had no one but me noticed his absence? Or, for that matter, his presence? My thoughts began to take a disturbing direction.

The following morning I asked the desk clerk if he knew the name of the tall man who had checked in at the same time I did. I gave as detailed a description as I could.

"Perhaps you mean Mr. Charles Digby, the missionary? He just returned from preaching to the aborigines for the last year. He checked out yesterday."

Digby! That was it! That was my man. But this explained everything and nothing. For the next week, I thought about the episode a great deal; the following week, much less; and, after that, hardly at all. By the time I returned to America, the man had almost vanished from my conscious mind but still returned occasionally to my dream world. The dream was always the same. He was in motion, and I was desperately trying to catch up with him in order to ask him something very important. However, he was either moving too fast or had vanished into a densely packed crowd. Once he turned around briefly and gave me a scornful look before vanishing.

Finally, even my dreams ceased. Several years passed, in the course of which I entirely forgot the entire episode. However, I may have seen him one more time. I was on a Delta Airlines flight from Las Vegas to Los Angeles. The flight was overbooked, and because I had arrived late, I would have been left behind if the airline had not been kind enough to let me take the last vacant seat in the first class section.

The stewardess led me to the vacant seat, and I sat down. The seat next to me was occupied by a man looking out the window, and I could not see his face. But then he turned his head toward me momentarily and nodded politely. As he did so, I felt a profound shock. For there sat my acquaintance from Australia and from church. The build and size were the same; the only changes were slightly greyer hair and a few more wrinkles. I needed only to hear his voice to be sure. It was not until we left the Sierra that I summoned the courage to ask him a direct question.

"Excuse me, sir. I wonder if we have met before. Are you a clergyman named Digby?"

He gave me a ironic look. The answer came in the sonorous voice I remembered so well.

"I'm terrible about names, especially my own. Call me Lazarus. I'm a teacher, although not a particularly successful one."

"What do you teach?"

"A good question. Let us say philosophy."

At this moment the plane flew out of a layer of clouds, exposing a scene of beauty so spectacular that I gasped. It was sunset, and we seemed to be descending down a long corridor lined with red and gold. At the end of the avenue the blue Pacific waited in silent splendor. Lazarus spoke again.

"In this world we are constantly surrounded by things of beauty, splendor, and grandeur. But we do not see them because we are wearing blinders. I try to persuade people to remove the blinders and behold the face of God. And now, if you'll excuse me, I would like to visit the men's room."

While he was gone, I tried to think about where I had heard the name "Lazarus" before. I knew it had some biblical significance, but what?

Somewhere between the Sierra and Los Angeles, I dozed off. When I awoke, the plane was approaching Los Angeles Airport. The seat next to me was empty. I waited for Lazarus to return from the men's room, but he never did, nor did I see him among the passengers collecting their baggage. Later I inquired if a Mr. Lazarus or a Mr. Digby had been among the passengers. I received negative replies in both cases. Then I remembered that Lazarus was the name of the man raised by Jesus from the dead.

Phoenix Street

Many of us have had at some time the sensation of being watched by an unseen observer. Usually there is no sequel and the incident is swiftly forgotten. But this is not always the case.

My only memorable experience of this kind occurred long ago when I was still a graduate student of biology in Cambridge, Massachusetts. I lived in a kind of boarding house run by a wistful Irish Catholic widow in her sixties who sublet several rooms in her part of a large subdivided house. It had once been elegant but was, by then, somewhat run down. The same could be said of Phoenix Street, on which the house was situated, and much of the neighborhood through which the street passed. Its heyday must have been around the turn of the twentieth century or even earlier.

I knew Phoenix Street only in the years not long after the second World War, when its decline was already visible. Back then Harvard graduate students were on their own in finding accommodations, and this was the best I could afford. The street was still dominated by large brick or brownstone townhouses that towered over it like a row of sleepy dowagers. Their interiors had been subdivided and now held multiple households. Here and there were gaps in the dignified facade of townhouses. These resulted from fires, which were frequent among the elderly buildings. They had never been replaced or had been replaced by cheaper and shabbier domiciles. Most of the business and professional people who had originally populated the street were long gone, replaced by a nondescript mixture of pensioners, students, clerks, and office workers. In perhaps the most telling index of change, families had been largely replaced by singles.

While the route of my daily walk to and from the university did not lie along Phoenix Street, I often walked along it to one of the cheap restaurants, where I got my greasy evening meal, or to reach the subway station, visit a store, see a movie, or sometimes just for exercise. The sidewalks were crowded only from about seven to nine in the morning and from five to seven in the evening, when people were heading either to or from the subway station.

At that time and place, few drove cars to work. Most used the subway even if they owned cars, which few did, since private car production had virtually ceased during the war and postwar production had not yet caught up with demand. In any event, apart from the periods when the leaving and returning swarms of humanity dominated the scene, the sidewalks were sparsely populated. Those who did travel them were largely students going to and from class, a few men who would be labeled today as "homeless," and a sprinkling of casuals, such as myself.

On the occasions when I went for a recreational walk with no specific objective, I preferred the daylight hours when the sidewalk was uncluttered. From November through March this usually meant from four to five in the afternoon and, in the balance of the year, from seven to eight. During the remaining daylight hours, I normally had other commitments, and I had avoided the area after dark ever since I had carelessly stepped on a pile of dirty cloth and heard it grunt.

"Where do you walk to?" asked Mrs. Kelly, my Irish landlady.

"Mostly just along Phoenix Street."

"Whatever for?"

"Partly for exercise and partly to look around. This is an interesting street."

"In daylight, you should be all right. At night it can get very interesting. The neighborhood has been going downhill ever since the Depression. I'm going to get out as soon as I can."

On this particular day at the end of November, I walked along Phoenix Street at about half-past four. Soon I would have to turn back if I wanted to avoid the early evening stampede of returning subway commuters. I regretted this, for I sorely needed the exercise. I had spent the day cooped up in my room, studying for one of the endless series of periodic examinations that Harvard inflicted upon its graduate students. My thesis research had stagnated, and I was badly worried. I began to wonder if I really belonged in biology or in science.

I was on the point of turning around when I paused, possessed by a distinct feeling of uneasiness. I sensed that I was being closely observed. The feeling was so overwhelmingly strong that it did not occur to me to question it. It was as if my reasoning powers had been momentarily overridden. My uneasiness was compounded by the even more irrational impression that whatever was watching me was malevolent and that a hostile will was beating down upon me.

I looked around but saw nothing to justify these sensations. I walked along a relatively undecayed portion of Phoenix Street. It seemed frozen in time, as if a gentleman in a frock coat and bowler hat might emerge from the door of one of the townhouses at any time. But no one did, and there were only two other people on the street. One was a plump Catholic priest on the other side who walked rapidly and looked preoccupied. On my side was an elderly man who I did not know but had seen before. He was walking a dog. Certainly they were not the source of whatever was disturbing me. My inner feelings must have shown on my face, for the dog-walking gentleman turned his head to look at me questioningly. This broke the spell, and I was able to exchange trivialities with him.

"You look like you could use a vacation," he said.

"Probably, but that would be unwise at this particular time."

"Harvard works its graduate students hard. Too hard."

"Do you speak from experience?"

"Yes, but it was long ago." His face darkened and he resumed his stroll.

I was calmed momentarily, but as soon as he walked on, the sensations returned, stronger than ever. In any event it was time to go back. As I turned to do so, I saw that there was indeed a face observing me closely—one which I had not noticed before. The townhouse closest to me had a large bay window behind which sat an old woman in a wheelchair facing the window. The reflection of the late afternoon sunlight from the glass was enough to obscure her image, unless I looked at a favorable angle, as I did now. I could see only part of the room, but I could make out that the furnishings were quite ornate. They clearly belonged to an earlier era. The wallpaper was of a complicated design, mostly black in color and quite as unusual then as it would be today. I could see several framed pictures, one of them apparently a portrait of a late nineteenth-century gentleman. Beside the woman's chair was a small table bearing a silver tray, a teapot, and a cup.

But it was the woman herself who held my attention. She was large and rather masculine in appearance, although somewhat eroded by age, with an expression stern and majestic. The immediate impression was one of strength and cold intelligence. She must have been very formidable once. The penetrating gaze with which she regarded me was not relaxed for a moment. It was as though she were about to burst out with a stream of imprecations. Her mouth twitched, as though she were trying to speak; but, if she made any sound, it did not penetrate the window. Just then a much younger woman in the uniform of a nurse's aide came into view. She bent over the older woman and then, after a sideways glance out the window, pulled the curtain shut. I must have been staring rudely.

The uneasiness and feeling of being watched vanished at once. I felt very chagrined during my walk home. If I were disturbed this much by a sick old woman, what would I do if I ever encountered a real menace? Probably I really did need a vacation. But that was out of the question. A vital cumulative examination was scheduled for the following week, and I was behind in my reviewing. So I set such thoughts aside and resolved to buckle down to studying.

When I got back, I questioned Mrs. Kelly.

"Do you know that very old woman who lives in a brownstone townhouse with a bay window about three blocks from here? She's confined to a wheelchair and has her own nurse." I went on to describe her as best I could.

"You must mean Mrs. Frank. She's the only one I know who fits your description. She's bad news. I never go near her if I can help it. Everyone thinks she murdered her husband many years ago. A few even think she's some kind of witch. I'd stay away from her if I were you."

This proved to be easier said than done. Although I never saw the woman again, she was not done with me yet. About a week later I had a compelling dream. I was once again walking along Phoenix Street past the row of undecayed brownstone townhouses. This time I had the street to myself with not a soul in sight.

In ordinary daytime life, where one can more or less do as one pleases, I would have either crossed to the other side of the street or made a 180-degree turn before I arrived there. But I was in dreamtime, where one does not necessarily do as one chooses. Down the street I went, right up to the house I remembered so well, with a mounting feeling of horror. The curtains were drawn and there was no sign of human activity, but I knew, as one does in dreams, that the woman was dying inside. I walked up the front steps and would presumably have knocked on the door or rung the bell if I had not awakened in a cold sweat and with a dry mouth. I had no desire to sleep again and spent the balance of the night studying.

After this, I made a point of avoiding that section of Phoenix Street in my walks. I would either walk in the other direction or make a detour around it. But about a week or so later, I was too preoccupied with other problems to notice where I was until I found myself walking past the very window where I had seen the woman. The curtain was not drawn and I could see clearly into the room, but there was no person in sight. I now noticed a prominent sign next to the front door. It said: "For Sale or Rent." The sign remained there for the remainder of my stay on Phoenix Street.

While I never saw the old woman again, even in a dream, I did hear her once more. Once again I was climbing the steps of her townhouse, but this time I opened the door and entered. Although I could not see her, I knew she stood nearby. When she spoke, it was in soft deadly tones. I cannot remember a single word of what she said, but her message was one of cold menace and approaching doom. It told me I had no future in my chosen field, I would never be anything but a failure, and I had nothing to look forward to but death.

The next morning I woke up in a suicidal depression accompanied by exhaustion, nausea, and diarrhea. I lay in bed all day in a state of prostration. By evening I seemed so sick that Mrs. Kelly, against my wishes, summoned a doctor. He ordered me into the university infirmary. The medical staff could not really diagnose my illness, which they realized was psychosomatic. In those days the catchall term was "nervous breakdown," although the doctors never used the phrase with me. It means incapacitating depression. For some time I tossed around in acute misery. In my dreams I often sensed the presence of the old woman, although I neither saw nor heard her.

My recovery was slow. I struggled against my depression and gradually improved. I found it was important to stay away from Mrs. Frank's house. If I passed by there, even unintentionally, I was likely to relapse. The trouble was I felt strangely drawn there, so that I had to exercise considerable vigilance whenever I was in the area. If I did this, the old woman left my dreams but continued to haunt my waking thoughts for a long time. It was many months before I was free from her visits. Meanwhile my graduate work took a turn for the better. I was helped by my decent and understanding research mentor, who cut me some slack until I was on my feet again. I ultimately got my degree and went on to a solid, if unspectacular, career.

Long afterward, in an altogether different life, I happened to be in Cambridge. Curiosity led me to risk revisiting Phoenix Street, which had been somewhat renovated. Mrs. Kelly's house was gone, but I found Mrs. Frank's still there. It had been converted into an acupuncture center, operated by two elderly Korean women. I felt no compulsion to enter but did so of my own free will. For the last time, I mounted the steps and opened the door. The interior looked perfectly ordinary; there was no black wallpaper. The women looked at me questioningly, but I simply smiled, excused myself, and retreated. There was no sequel to the visit. I was free from Mrs. Frank at last. Nothing lasts forever, not even evil.

THE SEASIDE WITCH

It was one of Maryland's rare near-perfect summer days. Ella and I were spending Labor Day 1980 at the beach. Our daughter Cathy, who had accompanied us in previous years, was traveling in Europe with a group from her college, so we were on our own. The chosen beach was Assateague Island, a park separated from Ocean City, Maryland, by an inlet, and one of the gems of the East Coast. One does not find here the swarms of rutting college students who overrun Ocean City itself in the summer months. Even on major holidays, the beach is shared only by a few sedate family groups. Avoiding even this sparse group only requires walking a hundred yards or so from the park headquarters in either direction to find perfect seclusion.

But on this particular day, perhaps because of below-average temperatures, the beach was even less crowded than usual, and we had set up our umbrella near one of the three lifeguard stands, which were manned by two collegiate youths and a girl. The water was calm and there was not much for them to do. So it was not surprising that they spent much of their time socializing rather than watching the bathers, who were few in number because of the cold water.

"Do you remember the first time we came here in 1960?" asked Ella.

"How could I ever forget that? I still shudder when I think of it."

"The place has changed a lot. The '67 storms washed all the old structures out to sea, including that horrible woman's cottage."

"I hope they took her along with it."

"It's much like any other beach now that the horseflies and mosquitoes are gone, and there's a bridge."

"It would have saved us a lot of grief if the bridge had been there in '60."

The afternoon was thoroughly uneventful. We passed it reading books and discussing Cathy's new boyfriend, of whom we were both suspicious. We were beginning to become bored when I noticed that the three lifeguards had stopped chatting and fixed their attention upon a point at the edge of the water about fifty yards down the beach. I looked that way too and at once saw what had drawn their notice. A man, one of the two remaining swimmers, was attempting to leave the water and walk onto the dry sand. He would have drawn attention anywhere, for he was both above average height, well more than six feet, and amazingly fat. He must have weighed at least five hundred pounds and resembled a somewhat out-of-condition sumo wrestler.

As we watched, all three lifeguards began to move toward the fat man, first slowly, then more rapidly, and then at a run. He was obviously in trouble, having sunk in the wet sand up to his kneecaps. He had apparently stepped onto a patch of quicksand or near-quicksand.

Quicksand arises from an upward flow of subterranean water through sand or mud. The upward flow reduces the effective density of the sand or mud to that of water, but the viscosity is of course much greater, so that a man struggling in it may be engulfed and drown, like a fly trapped in molasses. This was the first time I had encountered quicksand, which is not common on the East Coast. This was also the case for the knowledgeable people of whom I made inquiries. It was obviously of limited extent, for the lifeguards could approach within three or four yards without sinking into it. The fat man had been unlucky.

He was now clearly in serious difficulties. He was already in too deep to completely withdraw either leg and, when he attempted to do so, he drove the other leg down deeper. In this way, he had succeeded in submerging both legs up to the mid-thighs. This was getting serious. I set down my book and ran over to the fat man, who now attracted a crowd.

While he received a welter of conflicting advice, he acquired little useful assistance, certainly none at all from the lifeguards, who were utterly beyond their depth. One of them ran to the park headquarters, about a half-mile away, to look for a rope, while a second held out the tip of a furled beach umbrella in an unsuccessful attempt to pull him out. The girl ran back and forth and squawked, with no obvious plan.

I knew that even if I had a rope, I could never pull so much weight out of the sand. However, I also remembered that there was a sure and easy method for getting loose. It was a minute or so before it came to me and, in the meantime, the man had sunk almost to his waist.

"Don't struggle," I called. "Lie down and roll out."

The principle could not be simpler. By redistributing his weight over a large area, the effective force per unit area that was driving him down would be reduced to a small fraction of its former value—a problem in basic statics, which is also the basis of the trick whereby a fakir can lie on a bed of nails.

However, my words did not seem to penetrate. I repeated them, but he only shook his head and continued to struggle.

"All right then," I yelled. "Do it your way. And let me know when you strike New Zealand."

This got results. He lay as prone as he could, and the reduced weight on his legs enabled him to pull them loose. He was then easily able to roll out, becoming coated with a layer of wet sand in the process. He had difficulty getting to his feet, but finally did so, with some assistance from onlookers. I received a short burst of applause from the group, initiated by Ella, who had followed me. At this point a lifeguard came running from park headquarters carrying a coil of rope.

We returned to our umbrella. "You look pleased with yourself," said Ella. I was, but I only shrugged and resumed reading my book. About a minute or so later, I became aware that we were not alone. I looked up to behold the man I had helped.

"I didn't want to leave without thanking you," he said. It was only upon seeing him standing erect that I could fully appreciate how massive he was. Despite his grotesque appearance, I also sensed a solidity I had not detected before. There was still muscle beneath the fat.

"Don't give it a second thought," I said. "Glad to help."

"Have we met before?" he asked. "You seem familiar somehow."

I looked at him again, focusing on his porcine face, which was less distorted by fat than his body, but nothing came.

"I don't think so," I said, although something about him elicited a faint, teasing memory.

"Well, thanks again," he said and turned to leave. As he did so, I noticed a curious tattoo on one arm. It consisted of a wheel with spokes radiating from the center, but with the separation of two spokes abnormally shortened, giving the design an oddly disturbing effect.

My sense of having seen him before now became too compelling to ignore and dominated my thoughts for some time. Moreover, I felt that our contact had occurred long ago and had been brief but significant. But where? I felt I could rule out work; the man was too plebeian. It was certainly not the army; our age difference was too great. He didn't seem like the sort to be living in our suburb.

Finally, I gave up trying to place him and then, as often happens, the door in my memory on which I had pounded in vain now opened of itself.

It didn't happen until we were driving home when I announced to Ella:

"Now I remember! He was the guy who helped us that summer in 1960."

"Are you sure? I don't remember him as fat."

"He wasn't, then."

Details flooded back. Twenty years earlier, the bridge from the mainland to Assateague Island had not yet been built. The only way to get to the island was by a dilapidated ferry that made the twenty-minute trip every two hours. In the 1920s Assateague and Ocean City had been parts of the same island; their separation into distinct islands dated only from 1933, when the great hurricane of that year created the deep inlet dividing the two. In the late twenties, an ambitious developer had begun the creation of a seaside resort, but the hurricane, together with the Depression, had put an abrupt end to his plans, which progressed no further than the construction of a hotel and a handful of cottages.

In August 1960, Ella and I made our first visit to Assateague, together with our one-year-old, Cathy. We had been staying in Ocean City and become bored with it. Assateague appealed to us because of its unspoiled condition and also because of the small herd of wild ponies for which it was famous. By default, we drove our battered ten-year-old Plymouth onto the ferry and were conveyed across the bay. We got out of the car to get a better view. Ella held Cathy. An older man, with a worn and weather-beaten face, seemed to be looking at us with some concern.

"Are you sure you want to take that baby on the island?"

"Of course," I said. "Why not?"

"The horse flies and mosquitoes are pretty bad. They live off the wild horses. They'll eat you alive, if you let 'em. If you're determined to go on, I advise you to keep the baby in the car with the windows up. Also, the road's only good for about a mile and a half. If you go farther, you'll get stuck for sure, unless you have four-wheel drive."

"Thanks. We'll bear it in mind," I said, although I did not believe him. No one we knew at Ocean City had given us such a dire warning about the insect life, although one or two had mentioned flies and mosquitoes. Our map, which we did not know was obsolete, showed a paved road running right down the center of the island, all the way to the Virginia border.

The ferry captain, a wizened and deeply suntanned ancient, informed us that after a ten-minute wait, the boat would return to the mainland and, after an hour's wait there, return to the island for the final crossing of the day. If we missed that one, we would have to spend the night on Assateague.

"Which I do not recommend," he added.

Although we had noticed no biting insects on the ferry, we rolled up the windows after we docked and drove onto the landing. Allowing a twenty-minute safety margin, we had about an hour and a half to spend on the island. We had decided in advance that if in doubt, we would cut short our stay and return to the landing to await the boat for whatever time was required.

Like all wise resolutions, this one was easier to adopt than to carry out. The road was barely two lanes and contained many small potholes, which were not enough to impede us seriously. I drove very slowly; we had ample time to study the curious surroundings.

We seemed to be in a city from which all products of human activity had been removed, except for road signs and boundary markers, as well as two wooden buildings. One was large and nearby, the other was small and barely visible in the distance. The road signs left over from the failed development were mostly intact but very weather-beaten, like sad ghosts haunting the city that never was. The large building drew my attention at once. I recognized it as the abandoned hulk of the hotel built in the '20s, when the development of Assateague was gaining momentum. The paint had long ago been worn off its wooden structure, giving it the look of a derelict beached ship. About a dozen wild ponies grazed nearby.

I did not want to leave without photographing such a memorable sight, so I stopped the car, grabbed my camera, and walked toward the hotel. We did not dare to try driving over the sand, which the sparse grass had not hindered from drifting. I startled a pony, which set off at a fast trot.

I was wearing shorts and had not gone more than two dozen steps before I felt a strong burning and itching sensation, first on my thigh, then on both thighs, as well as my arms, lower legs, and neck. A downward glance showed that I was host to at least a dozen very large flies of a kind I had not seen before. Their bites drew substantial blood, so that my legs and arms became covered with blood when I swatted them. I did not begrudge them the blood, which I could easily spare, but they insisted on giving me something in return. This something made each bite itch and burn to an intolerable degree.

I returned to the car in double-quick time. Ella gasped when she saw me. Although my hands had been in constant motion, slapping the exposed parts of my body, I could not keep up with the flies, and by the time I reached the car, I was covered with blood and the carcasses of flies. I jumped inside and slammed the door. Three or four flies entered with me, one of which stung Ella, who screeched. But finally we dispatched them all, and I sat there breathing hard. The car seats were badly stained with blood.

"What shall we do?" I asked.

"Go back. Right now," said Ella. "Perhaps we can still catch the boat."

But we were too late, though not by much. The boat was about sixty yards off-shore; the captain waved to us, but kept on going.

"You bastard," I thought.

"Well, now what?" said Ella.

"As long as we're here, we may as well drive to the end of the paved road and get some pictures. I can't see just sitting here for an hour."

Ella shrugged resignedly. She hadn't wanted to come to Assateague in the first place. I photographed the old hotel as best I could from the car and then proceeded down the dilapidated road, doing my best to dodge potholes. Occasionally I stopped to photograph a wild pony. I now understood why their tails were in constant motion and why they were never still but were always twitching and fidgeting.

Apart from the old hotel and the single cottage in the distance that we had seen earlier, the only human signs were the battered road signs and what looked like the remains of a wrecked cottage here and there. Apparently, the hurricane had put an abrupt end to construction in its early stages. I had noticed earlier that the texture of the sand was very fine, which made it quite mobile in even a moderate wind. It had formed large dunes not far from the road. There was not enough grass to stabilize them, perhaps because of overgrazing by the ponies. In places the sand had drifted over the edge of the road, making it difficult to judge its boundaries.

Because I wanted to stay on the road at all costs, we traveled very slowly and almost twenty minutes had elapsed before we reached what I took to be the end of the useable section. Actually, there was no abrupt end. The potholes grew steadily more frequent and deep, while the asphalt portions shrank. When there seemed to be more potholes than pavement, I decided it was time to turn around, much to Ella's visible relief. Cathy had woken up and looked out the windows and then at me, questioningly.

However, there was a problem I had not foreseen. The asphalt had narrowed until it was only a little more than one lane wide. How could I turn around without going off the road? The wind had picked up and the blowing sand made it difficult to see.

I was unable to solve the problem. I could keep either my front or my rear wheels on the pavement, but not both. I decided to try to back up to where it was wider, but perhaps because of the poor visibility, I drove off the pavement, and both the rear wheels went in the sand. Here I came to a halt, with my rear wheels spinning helplessly and throwing up sand. Five minutes of lurching back and forth, which sometimes works in snow, produced no result except to drive us in deeper.

Ella's reaction was remarkably restrained.

"Now we are really in trouble," she said quietly.

"I'll try to dig us out," I said, without much conviction.

The sand was almost up to the hubcaps now. There was no shovel, or other digging tool, in the car. And, of course, there were still the flies. I thought of *Leiningen and the Ants* and his stopgap solution.

I remembered that in the back of the car was a pair of long pants, a long-sleeve shirt, and a cap. I put these on over my other clothes, tucking my pants legs into my socks, and wrapped a towel around my face and neck, using a pair of goggles to shield my eyes. Unfortunately, I had no gloves.

What would I dig with? Necessity is the mother of invention. (Invention has no father.) I easily ripped a road sign off its decayed post and began digging with that. After twenty minutes I saw I was getting nowhere; the blowing sand filled the hole faster than I could dig it out. At least I had felt no insect bites, perhaps because there were no ponies in sight.

Then I had what seemed like a good idea. The cottage we had earlier glimpsed on the horizon now lay about a quarter mile behind us. Also, someone was probably at home, for I could see what looked like a jeep sitting in front. Perhaps they would have a shovel we could borrow. If we were really lucky, they might give us a ride to the ferry, or use the jeep to pull us out of the sand.

For want of a better idea, I decided to walk to the cottage. I had only gone about fifty yards when I felt an insect bite on my ankle; the flies had gotten through my defenses. The second was not long in coming, followed by the third, fourth, and fifth, after which I lost count. But I gritted my teeth and soldiered on, having no promising alternative. By the time I reached the cottage I was in misery. I was not cheered by a glance at my watch, which told me that the ferry would leave in about twenty minutes.

Despite the presence of the jeep, the bedraggled cottage showed few signs of human activity. I thought I saw a curtain quiver, but I could not be sure. Nevertheless, having nothing to lose, I knocked on the door. There was no response, but I heard what sounded like a large dog barking inside. I knocked again, harder.

This time a face appeared at the window. It belonged to a woman in later middle age, who regarded me with such intense malice that I froze momentarily. Indeed I have never seen, before or since, a look of such concentrated hatred, most startling in a person never encountered before. Still, I did not have the impression that I was looking at a madwoman, but rather at a person still in possession of her faculties, which were now dedicated entirely to malevolence. It was a witch's face. I had a sensation of intense and penetrating cold that seemed to clutch at me.

My hopes faded, but she was still my best prospect. I pointed to our car and yelled that we were stuck in the sand and the last boat would be leaving soon.

She opened the window a crack and spoke in a lovely contralto voice.

"That is no concern of mine. I suggest that you leave my property before I set the dog on you."

The dog, which must have been very large, was now in a raging fury. I was so startled by the contrast between her voice and her appearance that it was a moment before I could collect myself enough to state,

"We only need a ride to the landing. It's not far, and we'll pay anything you ask. We have a baby with us and a night out here would be very hard on her."

What happened next would have been incomprehensible in any normal human context. She burst into exquisitely modulated laughter. If my eyes had been closed, I could have imagined I was listening to a scene from an operetta. The laughter stopped suddenly, and I heard the woman's voice again.

"You should have thought of that before you brought her out here. I suggest you leave while you can."

And with that she slammed the window shut. I heard the dog scratch at the door and decided to return to the car. I wondered if I was getting a foretaste of hell, which is said to be suffering in an atmosphere of mockery. The sensation of cold was very strong now.

There was now about fifteen minutes left before the ferry left. While the sand would slow me down, there was a chance I could make it if I was by myself, but I could never get Ella and Cathy there in time. We had no food and very little water. Ella and I could get through the night, but I worried about Cathy. She would certainly be badly dehydrated by morning.

However, I had not had my last surprise of the day. As I approached our car, I saw that we were no longer alone. A beach buggy with huge tires had stopped and two men had gotten out, one of whom was very tall and powerfully built, although starting to put on weight. As I watched in astonishment, he coolly lifted up the rear end of the car and set it on the asphalt. In the process the exposed parts of his body became covered with flies, which he ignored, not even bothering to brush them off. He grinned as he looked at my weird outfit. I noticed his unusual tattoo. When he spoke, it was very much to the point:

"We'll follow you to the landing. We had better not waste any time."

We made it to the ferry with five minutes to spare. I tried to thank the man properly, but he only made a dismissive gesture.

"Why are you on the island?" I asked.

"Fishing. What else?"

Then another question occurred to me.

"Do you know that woman who lives in the cottage?"

He was silent for a moment and an ambiguous look occupied his face.

"She's a leftover from the development that went bust. She lost all her money and it soured her on everything. She's bad news. I don't like to talk about her or even think about her if I can help it."

He paused for a few moments and then spoke again with a chuckle.

"We had words at our last meeting. She put a kind of curse on me. She said I would change into a human hog over a long period of time. I don't know what she meant."

I did not know what to say to this and did not pursue it.

So that was that; we spoke no more. The ferry soon landed, and we went our separate ways, to meet no more until two decades had passed and then under very different circumstances. Within a short period of time I had encountered unconditional malice and unconditional benevolence. Ella and I silently reflected for some time about what had happened and its bearing on the duality of human nature, but it gradually faded from our thoughts and then from our memories until reanimated by our latest meeting at the beach, in which our roles were reversed. People change with time, and their roles change with them.

When I placed the man in my memory after the second incident, I felt curiously relieved, as if a balance had been restored to the universe. I am still puzzling over the witch.

THE UNINVITED GUEST

Like most nightmares, this one began harmlessly enough. It was the week after Christmas 1980—New Year's Eve, in fact, shortly after the election of Ronald Reagan for president of the United States. I had driven from Baltimore, where I was a postdoctoral fellow in geophysics at Johns Hopkins, all the way to Lancaster, Pennsylvania, to capitalize on the last day of a spectacular post-Christmas sale of men's clothing. The results did not justify the trip. The material had been picked over, and I could find nothing in my size that I liked. Not wanting to leave empty-handed, I bought a blue blazer made in Romania that I did not really want. By the time I finished, it was already getting dark and clearly time to go. I noticed with little joy that patchy fog appeared here and there.

Even apart from my unsuccessful mission, I was not in the best of moods. Christmas is always a time of summing up and self-appraisal, and the year had not been good. It is also a time of comparisons, when winners gloat quietly over losers. I was not helped by the fact that my older brother, with whom I had little in common except for being half-Korean, was achieving early and spectacular success in his own field, while I was essentially treading water in mine. Our father had always compared me unfavorably with my brother, saying I lacked the prerequisites for success, especially ambition and drive.

My morose sentiments were enhanced by the fact that what had seemed like a severe cold showed signs of going over to something more serious, perhaps the exotic flu, which had been raging all winter. In any event, I had a fever and felt very tired. I decided I had better forget about the New Year's Eve party my boss was throwing and just try to get back home safely and go to bed. Alcohol was certainly the last thing I needed.

Such were the gloomy thoughts that occupied my mind as I approached the Susquehanna Bridge. I was recalled to reality by the realization that it was now quite dark and the fog was getting steadily thicker. I would have to drive slow now and might be very late getting home. Happily, there was no snow on the ground. My problems were compounded by the sight of a stopped police car with flashing lights and a cop who directed all traffic to a two-lane, blue highway. This more or less paralleled the river as it flowed to the east. Apparently, there had been an accident on the bridge.

Ordinarily I love the gentle and beautiful Susquehanna, which has never gotten the attention from artists and writers it deserves. But on this particular occasion, I would have given a good deal to be ten miles past it and heading south on I-83. As it was, I would have to go many miles out of my way to take the I-95 bridge, and I was feeling sicker by the minute. Moreover, the fog, which seemed to spill over from the river, soon became so dense that I had to slow to first twenty, and then fifteen, miles per hour to avoid overrunning my headlights. My night vision is poor at best, and I would have been uncomfortable even without the fog. It was the worst sort of fog—the wet, heavy kind that soaks down to your soul and makes a long dreamless sleep seem the best of states.

Thirty minutes later, I crept along at ten miles per hour, just barely able to see the edges of the narrow road. I could detect approaching cars only at the last minute. One of these, which was going much too fast and straddling the center line, barely missed me. I drove thereafter with my wheels skirting the edge of the pavement.

I was now lost. I should have passed through several small towns, but I had not seen a single town or even a single lighted house since I began the detour. I must have somehow made a wrong turn in the fog. I pulled off the road and got out my map, but a map is only useful if you know roughly where you are. There seemed to be only two options. I could park where I was and try to sleep until morning, or I could keep on going blindly and hopefully stumble on some outpost of civilization.

I had no difficulty deciding in favor of the latter course. I distrusted my illness, which was getting steadily worse. Moreover, I did not like where I was. Even in the dark, localities can have intrusive personalities. There was something distinctly disturbing, even menacing, about this one, although I would have been at a loss to explain exactly what bothered me. So I drove on, recognizing with some dismay that my gas tank was getting low and I probably did not have enough to get back to Baltimore.

Road traffic seemed to have increased; all of it in the direction I was going and, for the most part, going much faster than I. I was passed by one car after another, many of them glittering rich man's cars: Mercedes, BMWs, Porsches, Cadillacs. Several were chauffeured limousines. They did not seem to have any regard for the fog or to care what they might run into or over.

It seemed like I had been driving a long time, but probably only about five or ten minutes elapsed before I noticed a diffused patch in the fog that transformed into a brilliantly illuminated building as I approached. The other cars pulled off the road and parked in a large graveled space in front of what the thinning fog allowed me to see was a large and elaborate mansion—a style popular in the '20s. After hesitating a moment, I followed them and parked my nondescript Chevette on the edge of the space, halfway in the grass. I should at least be able to locate my car easily.

As I got out of my car, I heard a scurrying of small feet in a nearby patch of high grass. There was a pause, and I saw momentarily two small luminous eyes staring at me. Then the eyes vanished, and I saw the back of a small furry animal with a long bald tail slink away in flight.

I trailed behind a small group who walked to the front door that a servant was holding open. A beam of light illuminated me as well as the elegant set with whom I tagged along. I could not help being impressed by the opulence of the dress of men and women alike, as well as by their failure to show even a peremptory recognition of my existence. But why should they? These were obviously rich people, probably not accustomed to take much notice of such a plebeian type as I. However, I began to wonder uneasily about what kind of reception I could expect inside.

They spoke typical rich people's chatter.

"Isn't it wonderful about the election?"

"It certainly is. I feel like I'd returned to my own country after a long exile."

As the last of those preceding me entered, the servant began to close the door, and I barely squeezed in. He made no move either to assist or to stop me. It was as if I were not there. However, I wondered if it might not be better if I left as quietly as I had come. What I saw overwhelmed me. The mansion was huge and more ornate than anything I had ever seen. Exquisite woodwork, parquet floors, and gold and marble fixtures were everywhere, as was the aroma of fine food and drink. It was a moment before I could grasp what I was looking at sufficiently to see it properly. While servants removed the overcoats of my erstwhile companions and presumably stored them in a cloakroom, no one offered to help with mine. Neither did anyone want to know who I was nor did they question the appropriateness of my being there. Finally, feeling somewhat chagrined, I hung my coat on a small rack I saw near the door and paused to look about me.

I was in a kind of foyer that was flanked on both sides by large rooms filled with people. In front of me, a magnificent marble spiral staircase led to the upper stories. The ceiling of the vestibule was very high and from it dangled a splendid crystal chandelier. Guests continually arrived and passed through the foyer into one of the rooms to the right or left. Their appearance fully harmonized with the upscale character of the house. The men wore evening clothes. The clothing of the women was exquisitely designed and obviously very expensive, although a little old-fashioned, and set off their handsome features very well.

In a large group, one expects to see at least a few who are fat or ugly or at least ordinary looking. But there was none of that here. Although many of the guests seemed to be in middle age, or even older, they all seemed tall, fit, and healthy, as well as uniformly elegant and patrician. Many had suntans, despite the season. They all seemed to speak with an accent, which I could not place. It was rather surprising to find that their voices were slightly high-pitched, even squeaky.

Moreover, all, even the oldest, seemed nimble and overflowing with nervous energy. I was especially struck by the incessant rapid twitching motion of their eyes and nostrils, which seemed never at rest, but always seemed to try to seek out or sniff out something of interest. The general impression their faces gave was of pride bordering on arrogance, but also with an elusive hint of vulgarity. None of them showed the slightest interest in me. The constantly searching eyes never rested on me for even an instant, even when I had a fit of coughing.

But this was neither here nor there. My reason for entering the house uninvited was to find out where I was so I could resume my drive home. I walked into the room to the left of the foyer, hoping to find someone approachable enough to explain my predicament to. While the room was crowded, there was no one who seemed accessible. Everyone appeared to be part of a group and engaged in animated conversation. My efforts to get attention by clearing my throat or saying "excuse me" were unsuccessful.

I noticed a marble bar on which sat a set of glasses and a large bowl of what looked like wine punch, which the guests were helping themselves to freely. Next to it was a small table laden with hors d'oeuvres of various kinds. Some looked like caviar, others like sushi, but most I could not recognize. The bartender took no more notice of me than anyone else. In my frustration, I recklessly poured myself a glass of punch and ate an hors d'oeuvre. I must not have been thinking clearly, for normally I find free-loaders repellent. The hors d'oeuvre was delicious, but so spicy that I had difficulty getting it down. The punch, however, was excellent, although slightly aromatic, and seemed very potent, as if it had been fortified. It took effect quickly, as I rarely drank alcohol, even a glass of beer, and I was also sick.

I now noticed a grey-haired man standing by himself who seemed different from the other guests. He was more modestly dressed and did not display their frenetic nervous activity. His face was gentle and refined and free from hubris. Moreover, while he did not speak, he regarded me closely with a friendly smile and even nodded, as if to assure me that he did not share the indifference of the others to my existence. Surely he was the person to help me. However, at this moment my attention was distracted by a burst of loud laughter from a hilarious group behind me, and when I turned back, the friendly stranger was gone. I did not quite have all my faculties. The punch was already having a significant effect, and it plus my illness seemed to act synergistically. However, it did momentarily seem to make me bolder and less intimidated by my surroundings.

I sighed and rejoined the nearby group, resolving to break in whenever their conversation faltered. This was going to be difficult, as the group I joined consisted of about a dozen individuals, all talking at once very rapidly and loudly, so much so that it was at first difficult for me to make any sense of the chaotic sounds. However, by focusing my attention upon two or three individuals who seemed to display, in exaggerated form, common characteristics and by trying to tune out the others as best I could, it became possible to catch at least snatches of what was being said. One could not call it a conversation. One thing, at least, was abundantly clear. The group, as well as the guests in general, were in a state of intense, almost delirious, jubilation, which owed little to the alcohol they had consumed.

"It's our turn again and this time nothing can stop us. If we let it slip through our fingers this time, we deserve to have our butts kicked."

"What happened last month has completely changed the situation. Very soon the good times will begin to roll in earnest. No one will ever want the sixties or seventies back."

"As long as we control the media, there's no reason we can't rule forever."

"And that's not all. The Soviet Union committed suicide when it installed Brezhnev and kept him so long. They'll fold up in a few years, and then there'll be no other force in the world strong enough to stop us. We'll rule, not just here but everywhere. Why settle for part when we could have it all?"

"It's supremely important to have the media in our pocket. That's going to cost, but it's worth it."

"There'll still be elections, but they won't mean anything. The candidates not on our side no one will ever hear of ..."

"We won't need secret police or concentration camps. With unlimited funds, we can co-opt all the smart people and make sure that only our point of view is ever heard ..."

What on earth were they talking about? And who were they? The allusion to the preceding November seemed to imply that the election of 1980 was a factor. But how? Some of what they said seemed to echo the sentiments of one wing of the newly victorious Republican party, but much went far beyond that.

Enough. I stepped into the middle of the group and said in a near-shout:

"Excuse me. I'm lost and I wonder if anyone could tell me where we are?"

The effect on the group was magical. The loud voices fell silent and all heads were turned in my general direction. Their faces were as arrogant as ever, and an element of exasperation had been added. The eyes had lost their nervous random movement and now searched slowly back and forth, as if trying to identify an invisible source of irritation, such as a sudden bad smell. However, they looked past or through me rather than at me. I now became aware of the friendly stranger I had seen earlier, who was now by my side. He grabbed me by the arm and pulled me away, placing his other hand over my mouth. Not till we were in an empty corner did he speak and then only in whispers.

"Don't do that again, for God's sake. Listen, if you must, but don't try to speak to them. They almost found you this time. Incidentally, here is where you are."

He drew a crude map, in which our current location was marked with an X.

"The wind is picking up, and I recommend that you postpone your departure until the fog clears, which should be in an hour or so. While you're here, listen to them, if you must, but don't try to talk to them. If you talk loudly enough they can notice you and, if they do, you will be sorry. That was a close call you just had. By the way, I would go easy on this punch."

"Who are they? And what is the matter with them? Are they crazy?"

"If you haven't guessed yet, you probably will in due course. But if you do, do not, at all costs, name them out loud. Ever. Also I would not stay too long. I would certainly get out before midnight."

Meanwhile, I noticed that the guests had abandoned their staring in my general direction and resumed, with shrugs, their conversation, which was, however, less animated and less uninhibited than before.

"It's very important not to move too fast, especially in the beginning. We can still blow everything."

"Like we did before?"

"Yes, like we did before."

"It will take time to change the mass mind, but it can be done. It's in a receptive mood now."

The group began to disperse and distribute themselves among the other circles, which were continually breaking up and reforming. My unknown friend had vanished again, leaving me utterly perplexed by what he had said and wondering how seriously I should take it. I was not helped by the fact that I was beginning to be slightly groggy and did not have all my wits.

One thing was for sure. Whatever prevented these strange people from acknowledging my presence, it was clear that prospects of friendly interaction between us were not bright. At the least they were certainly the worst snobs I had ever seen. I decided that it would be wise to follow the advice I had been given and assume they were dangerous. Nevertheless, I felt curiously drawn to them and very inquisitive about what they were talking about.

I selected another cluster at random, this time standing well away from them, so that I could understand even less than before. Several of these were in uniform. I kept hearing the words "bases, military presence, security, gulf," and, above all, "oil, oil, oil." It was not hard to surmise the general drift of their conversation, but capturing the details was hopeless.

I shifted to a smaller group who spoke more slowly and I could understand better. I was also assisted by the fact that they spoke in turn rather than all at once. The members of this cluster seemed to have an academic background and spoke more formally than the others. I could also grasp that their topic was sociological in nature and that there was little divergence of opinion. This conversation appeared to be dominated by a very tall individual, whose face seemed particularly hard and cold. His speech was quite formal, even pedantic. I present here only his general drift.

"All our troubles come from the fact that the national standard of living has been allowed to become unrealistically high relative to the rest of the world. This is a natural result of the leveling tendencies of the last half-century, which have shrunk the differential of wealth between the highest and the lowest to a dangerous degree. It is precisely this differential that drives the masses to work to produce wealth which they will never see ...

"If we want to restore the differential, it will be necessary to get rid of the unions or shrink their power. There are two things working in our favor. Mass higher education has enabled their most able and intelligent members to rise from the working to the managerial class. The actual running of the unions has increasingly been assumed by criminals, who have tended to discredit the whole idea of organized labor ...

"It will also be important to eliminate the barriers to free trade, especially with third world countries. This will enable us to shift much of our manufacturing base to places where the wage level is low and will tend to force down the cost of labor here ...

"Finally, and most importantly, we must remove the floor that has been supporting the lowest, non-working class. I am referring, of course, to welfare and food stamps. If our bargaining position is to be strong, it is essential that the lower strata realize there is no limit to how low they can sink. Social Security and Medicare will, of course, have to go too, although this will take time ...

"As real income falls, the slack will be taken up by the entry of women into the labor market. As it becomes the norm for wives to work, family incomes will be stable, or even rise a little, *at first*. This will, for a long time, conceal what is really happening ....

"The lowering of taxes will release a flood of money for investment. This will produce a burst of prosperity. However, the fruits of this prosperity will not be dissipated wastefully among all levels, as in the past, but focused upon the most productive members of society. This will restore a profoundly biased distribution of wealth and guarantee a very steep gradient of wealth between the highest and lowest. This gradient will be self-sustaining, as it will provide a maximum incentive to achievement. The most able will move rapidly to the top, while the least able will sink lower and lower. We will have a genuine meritocracy at last, where wealth is directly correlated with productivity. There will never be another revolution, because the people capable of leading it will have been co-opted into the ruling class."

Against my better judgment, I helped myself to another glass of punch and then walked into another room, which was quite as elegant as the one I had left, although smaller. It contained a large marble fireplace in which several large logs were blazing. Two guests, who stood apart from the others, seemed to be discussing the death penalty. I was by now in no condition to follow their talk in detail, but something like the following was said, in the curious tones and accents typical of the guests.

"It's not central to our system, but it's important all the same. It is, in fact, the final brick that completes the structure. As the number of submen packed into the lowest strata becomes greater and greater and they turn increasingly to crime, they will begin to exert a destabilizing effect, unless they are removed systematically."

"Of course. First we must revive capital punishment for murder. There is least resistance to that. When it is firmly established and being carried out efficiently and systematically, it will be time to extend it, first to other forms of homicide and then to all violent crimes. While it will take time and we must move carefully, it will then be appropriate to extend it to repeating felons who have more than a maximum—say three—number of convictions. The final step, where it blends with euthanasia, will be the extension to those who are incapable of supporting themselves or contributing in a meaningful way to society because of age or disability. For such people there is clearly a duty to die and get out of the way of the more productive elements of society."

"There is a practical consideration as well. The occurrence of a large number of deaths of healthy individuals means the availability in unlimited numbers of organs suitable for transplants. This means that those qualified by wealth and status for replacement parts may have access to an indefinite extension of life. No longer will death be the great leveler and neutralizer of success."

This was too much. It was all I could do to keep silent. I walked quickly away from them and attached myself to the periphery of another group, who seemed of a less practical and more philosophical bent than the others.

"If we are to have a world with no fetters on competition or progress, then we will have to promote selfishness from a vice to a virtue, so that it will be taken for granted that each individual will pursue his own interests to the exclusion of all other considerations. Once this is accepted as common knowledge, it will enormously simplify life in general. It will be unnecessary to lie about one's motives for one thing. Hypocrisy will vanish, as will the archaic idea of *good* and *evil*. Human behavior will become predictable."

"Then we must of course get rid of the ancient and peculiar notion that each individual is somehow responsible for his fellows and owes them something, quite apart from any *quid pro quo*. This aberration is linked to and perhaps inseparable from the traditional Christian view of the world. However, Christianity is dying and Judaism is not far behind it. Already scholars are beginning to speak of the 'post-Christian era.'"

"The death of religion will free us from the wasted emotion of guilt and from the debilitating idea of sin. The foolish idea of 'love', which has caused so much grief, is already withering away. When these are gone, we shall be free in the whole sense of the word. There will be nothing to interfere with the competitive principle, whereby wealth, power, and pleasure are parceled out to the strongest."

Here they parted company completely with the conservative Republicans and indeed with nearly all philosophers, except perhaps Nietzsche and Ayn Rand. I had heard this line of thought before in late-night bull sessions as a student. Pain and grief must always exist to complement pleasure and give it meaning, just as Christianity demands hell to balance heaven.

I thought hazily of Michelangelo's Last Judgment, which the world these people were sketching would resemble, except that it would be the strong rather than the virtuous who rose and the weak rather than the evil who sank. Life would be perpetual warfare over the right to press endlessly on the nerves of pride, power, and pleasure. But surely it was all just a lot of talk.

I drifted shakily over to another small circle, where the topic seemed to be education. I began to find it difficult to follow the conversation for any length of time or even to stand upright. The meaning of what I heard became blurred, recovered lucidity for a time, and then faded again, like listening to an old-fashioned shortwave radio with much static.

"Universal free public education must go. This is very central to ensuring that the gradient of wealth and power parallels that of knowledge and sophistication, as well as ability. Above all, higher education must be restricted. There must never again be anything like the GI bill."

I could have predicted it. They, of course, recognized that this change must be gradual. Funding for public schools would be gradually reduced, so that their quality would progressively decline. The best students would transfer to private schools. In the intermediate stages, they would be supported by some form of vouchers, the issue of which would become progressively more restricted. Finally, the remaining public schools would deteriorate to the point where they would not be worth going to and could be gradually phased out.

I began to sense a mounting danger and wanted badly to get out of there. I looked out a window and saw that the fog had indeed thinned. I decided to chance it, although by this time I was hardly in a good condition to drive. But now I heard a peal of female laughter coming from a large room deeper in the house. I now noticed that, while the numbers of men and women entering had seemed roughly comparable, there had been only a minority of women in the rooms I had passed through. They must be largely concentrated in one or more of the other rooms. Curiosity led me to enter the large room from which the feminine laughter had come. As I did, I looked at my watch. I was shocked to see that it was almost eleven o'clock, so that I must have been there almost four hours. Impossible. There must be something wrong with the watch or with me.

My surmise was correct. The room was indeed full of women with a few men. They were all handsome and graceful, even the oldest, and many of them were ravishing, but in a special way. No one would have called them merely pretty. There was a feral and predatory quality to their beauty, like that of a lioness poised to spring. Like their male counterparts, they were full of restless energy, although their jubilation was more subdued. But what they had to say was even more shocking than what I had heard earlier.

"The best of it is that we are finally losing the terrible burden of *goodness*, which always fell disproportionately upon the female sex. To be afflicted with this is not only a handicap in every meaningful endeavor but also an obstacle to most pleasures. Goodness has always gone hand in hand with such idiotic notions as sin, love, and guilt. When this idea is finally gone forever, we can begin to be truly free."

"I suppose that by 'we' you mean the members of the ruling class?"

"Of course. Being free means that you always get your way. It's impossible for this to be true for everyone at the same time. Total freedom for the few means total servitude for the many. Liberty and equality are not friends and cannot coexist."

Her views did not quite stand up to analysis, and I wished that I dared break my silence. The second glass of punch I had recklessly drunk was now getting to me in earnest. I began to feel dizzy and confused. One of the women laughed loudly and I got a glimpse of her mouth. It seemed to me that there was something odd about her teeth, but before I could pinpoint what it was, my attention was distracted by a call for attention in the large room I had quitted earlier, followed by silence.

An announcement was about to be made. Everyone in my room now rushed out to join the others, with the exception of one woman who had stood somewhat apart from the crowd and seemed preoccupied with her own thoughts. She was as beautiful as the others, but there was an introspective and somewhat morbid quality to her beauty. Finally, after everyone else had left, she walked slowly toward the door.

Unfortunately, I had got between her and the door, thinking to go back outside to my car to try to sleep. She walked right into me, feeling much heavier than she looked. We both fell down, with her in a kneeling position on top of me. I expected an outraged scream, but instead she silently stood up and regarded me fixedly for a moment, looking me up and down. Then her face became contorted, first with an ambiguous smile and then with delirious, squeaky laughter.

Meanwhile I struggled to get up. She was sober in an instant and then helped me to my feet, beckoning me to follow her in the direction of the staircase. When I hesitated and stumbled, she grabbed my hand and pulled me along. How strong she was!

I was rapidly losing what remained of my faculties and was finding it difficult to stand erect, much less attempt to reason with my abductress. Somehow we must have got upstairs and into a bedroom. Then, for the first time, she spoke, her squeaky voice seeming inconsistent with her voluptuous form.

"You're lucky it was I who found you. I've always wanted to get in bed with one of you. Too bad you're drunk."

I remember only patches of what happened after that. I believe that we got our clothes partially off and that she had draped herself over me. I seem to remember she was kissing my neck when there were sounds of turmoil downstairs and someone seemed to be calling to her. The kiss turned into a savage bite that drew blood. The next minute, she was gone. Shortly after that I was unconscious, which is not to say that my brain was inactive. In fact, I had the most vivid dream I can remember.

What I dreamed of was rats. They swarmed in great numbers all around me and even ran over me. They seemed to have an objective and ran in the same general direction. Although a particular rat might move around erratically, in the end he always joined in the rush to the common destination, whatever that was. It was like the climax in the H. P. Lovecraft story *The Rats in the Walls*, except that the rats were not in the walls but all over me. Occasionally a rat would pause and look back at me but without malice, in a kind of half-invitation.

They were clearly no ordinary rats. They were large and fat, and their fur was smooth, thick, and glossy, while their eyes were bright and mobile—in short, all that an animal should be. They would certainly have been out of place among the miserable specimens to be found in the back alleys of the inner city. Strangely enough, although I had always feared and loathed rats, I felt no trace of either emotion. Indeed, I sensed a curious desire to jump up and join them in their quest, whatever that might be.

But this was not to be. The dream faded, and I lapsed back into outer darkness. When I awoke, it was broad daylight, and I was cold sober, although with a terrible headache and feeling very weak. I found myself on the floor in a small bedroom, lying on a shabby rug. I was fully dressed, although somewhat disheveled. I went to a mirror and looked at my neck and shoulders. There was not a mark on me. The house was very silent; there were no sounds of human activity at all. I looked out the window to find that the fog was gone and there was not a cloud in the sky. It was what is sometimes called a fine winter's day.

I left the bedroom and went down the steps as softly as I could, expecting every moment to encounter an irate house owner ready to confront me as an intruder. I was struck by the fact that the house was very ordinary, just a modest country dwelling. There was no trace of the opulence I dimly remembered from the preceding evening. There was still no sign of anyone about, and there was a certain deadness in the air that suggested a vacant house. I looked for the coat I had hung up the night before, but it was nowhere in sight. I did not want to press my luck, and I walked as quickly as I could over the worn carpet and out the front door. There was no car but my own, parked incongruously at the edge of an empty and somewhat weedy lot.

Somehow I got to my car and drove back to Baltimore without further incident, except that I was surprised to find after I got there that Blossom, a neighbor's large calico cat with whom I had always been on the best of terms, now went mad at the sight of me. Her fur puffed out and she bolted. Since then I have never been able to get a cat to stay in the same room with me. I seem to have lost my canine friends as well, although the effect is less dramatic. I have never told anyone about my adventure, not even my wife—especially not my wife.

Incidentally, time has proven my father wrong. I turned out to be a perfectly successful member of the family with no need to feel inferior to my brother.

Some years later, quite by chance, while driving through southeastern Pennsylvania I found myself on a secondary road that seemed familiar. Presently I came upon an isolated house that caught my attention at once. A reference to my map confirmed that it could only be—not the house I had come to—the house I had left on New Year's Eve 1980. I parked my car near where I had placed it long ago, walked to the front door, and rang the bell. A nice brown-eyed and grey-haired lady in early old age answered the bell. She was mildly surprised by my questions but answered them gracefully.

"Yes, we've lived here about twenty-five years. We're here all year long, except that we usually visit our married daughter in Arizona over Christmas and New Years.

"You must mean the Fellner mansion. It was located right where we are, but it's been gone a long time. They say it was really something. It burned down around 1930 and what little was left was dug up and removed. After the war, someone tried to develop the land, but this was the only lot sold. People were scared of the place for some reason. We got our lot dirt cheap."

I thanked her and left. I saw no rats, not even the everyday variety.

THE PILGRIM

The comatose body of Herbert Fleming lay on a gurney in his private recovery room, although it was clear that in his case, there would be no recovery. He was still a striking man who commanded the attention of everyone who passed by him. Barbara, his daughter and sole surviving relative, sat by the bed, where she had been for hours. Occasionally, she thought she could detect a tremor, giving rise to the hope that he might regain consciousness momentarily—long enough for them to exchange a few words. This seemed very important to her, although they had not spoken or communicated for years and had not gotten along for many years before that.

"He looks like he is dreaming," said the nurse.

"I hope they are pleasant dreams," said Barbara. "He deserves them. He wasn't very lucky in life."

"A book that helps me at times like this is *The Great Divorce* by C. S. Lewis."

"I've heard of it, but I've never read it."

"He describes the Hereafter as an endless walk higher and higher into majestic mountains."

"And the climb ends in Heaven?"

"It's not spelled out, but that's the implication."

Barbara had flown in from San Francisco and rushed to the hospital as soon as she had been informed of her father's accident. Apparently, Professor Fleming, who was already suffering from inoperable cancer, had absent-mindedly stepped off the curb to retrieve a dropped copy of the *New York Times*. He had thereby placed himself in the path of an oncoming car that struck him from behind—the sort of thing elderly people are prone to do.

"He never knew what hit him," the emergency room doctor had said.

From time to time she got up and paced nervously or went outside for a cigarette. It had been clear from the onset that there was no hope whatsoever, and the physicians had offered none. While Herbert had lingered much longer than expected, he had never regained consciousness and had given no sign of recognition. After Barbara had been there for five hours, the nurse suggested gently, "Why don't you go to the lounge and try to get some sleep? We'll come get you if there's any change."

"All right, but I want to be called if there's even the slightest change." She left for the lounge. When the nurse was sure Barbara was gone, she left herself, turning out the light.

When Herbert regained self-awareness, he seemed to be alone in a dark room, empty except for a few pieces of nondescript furniture, including a full-length mirror. The only source of light was a kind of night light sitting on a worn-looking table. Although he felt very tired and weak, he somehow evoked the strength to walk to the mirror. Sick as he felt, nothing had prepared him for the aged and emaciated apparition that looked back at him.

Good God! he thought. *Is that me?* He had as yet no idea of where he was, how he got there or even who he was. He pressed his eyelids tightly closed and then reopened them, but the image in the mirror did not change.

He was certain of only one thing: it was terribly urgent to get out of that room. Although every step caused him pain and required a conscious effort, he somehow managed to cross the room, pass through an open door, and stumble down a short set of steps without falling, although the margin was not great. He now found himself in a darkness that was not quite total. There was no moon, but the sky was cloudless and the stars, which were grouped in curious and unfamiliar constellations, were bright. Also, there was a very faint glow from a part of the horizon, which he took to be the east. As he stood with his back to the door from which he had just emerged, the light sufficed to show a rather narrow path. It stretched before him for a significant distance before dipping into what seemed to be a shallow valley filled with what looked like a churning and luminous fog. While he could not see the terrain on either side of the path very clearly, it was obviously quite rough. He could make out piles of jagged rocks, punctuated by what seemed to be dense bushes with many thorns. In his weakened condition he had only two choices. He could return to the place he had left or he could proceed along the path.

He did not hesitate long before choosing the path, rejecting out of hand a return to the room. He had planned to walk at first only about a hundred feet to a rock outcropping, where he could sit and rest for a while. However, to his surprise, he found that his condition seemed to improve slightly as he walked. In particular, he no longer seemed in imminent danger of falling. He therefore extended his walk somewhat before stopping to rest, thereby putting more distance between himself and the room.

Until now he had been too preoccupied with placing one foot ahead of another and keeping his footing to think seriously about his condition. But now a swarm of questions beset him. First of all who was he? What was his name?

Whatever his past occupation had been, it must have trained him to think systematically, for he approached the problem logically. He would begin with the first name. Starting with the As, he considered Abraham, Albert, Alfonso, Alfred, Anthony, Arthur, … Ashley, … Nothing evoked even the faintest signal of recognition. Then it was the turn of the B's: Barney, Bartholomew, Basil, Baxter, Bertram, Bill, … Again, nothing. In this way he went over each of the letters in turn. Only the Hs gave him the slightest encouragement: Hal, Harold, Harry, Henry, Herman … And now his frustration became intense, as it seemed that what he sought was barely beyond the reach of his awakening memory. Heinz? Heinrich? No it wasn't a foreign-sounding name. Homer? Horatio? No, now he was getting further away. He rubbed his forehead and felt more tired than ever. Herbert? *Herbert*? Of course, of course, of course; that was it. He was Herbert. But Herbert what? Let it go for now. His alphabetic approach would never work for the legion of possible surnames. Perhaps even one retrieved fact could provide a nucleus about which the rest of his memory could crystallize. Nucleus? Crystallize? Where had he gotten these words? He had a frustrated feeling that he had half recovered what he desired from the quicksand only to have it slip from his fingers and sink back into the morass.

His head seemed to hurt. He rubbed it and stood up. It was time to walk again. His brief rest had done him good, and he seemed to stand more erect and walk faster. It was not long before he stood on the outskirts of the shallow valley, where he paused in some confusion. As he had no idea what he was looking at, he did not really see it. Instead, he had to replace the actual image with the closest and least irrational item he could summon from his internal data files. What he had taken for a luminescent mist was clearly nothing of the sort but rather the incredibly complicated interior of a building that had no exterior. What had seemed like fog had coalesced into an endless series of walls, rooms, and corridors, which were well-lit, mobile, and semi-transparent and which overlapped and intermeshed in a bewildering way. He would have hesitated to enter, had it not been for the fact that the path was still there and very visible. It led right into the chaos, stretching through and out of it on the other side.

Once inside, he became aware not only of inanimate shapes but also of humanoid images that milled about and passed in and out of his field of vision. He found moreover that if he selectively focused his attention upon a restricted zone, the aimless motion seemed to abate, and the humanoid and other blurred shapes within the zone appeared to coalesce, becoming less transparent and more visible and recognizable. Now he could see that the humanoids wore two kinds of costume. Some wore what looked like green pajamas; others, who seemed to be female, wore white dresses. He further observed that the green pajama people were clustered about what appeared to be a kind of table and they seemed very busy. As he watched, one of them, who seemed to be in authority, stood upright from what had been a stooped position and slowly shook his head. None of the figures paid Herbert any heed.

Herbert's curiosity was now sufficiently aroused to overcome his weariness and apathy, and he stepped toward the vision, but as he advanced, it retreated, and when he relaxed his attention momentarily, it collapsed into the original chaos. He tried to concentrate again, but the effort seemed to hurt him, and he soon abandoned it and turned to return to the path. Although he thought that he had taken only one or two steps, the path had retreated a significant distance, and he had to walk for some time to regain it. With his attention focused on the path rather than his surroundings, the latter became more inchoate than ever and soon lost all resolution. Herbert resolved that henceforth he would stick to the path, come what may, and resist all temptation to stray.

Herbert sensed, in the absence of proof, that what he had passed through and now emerged from was a place where he had been, but which he had never seen. Moreover, it seemed to be a hospital and to have figured in his recent past. Beyond this, his speculations made little progress and began to lead him down gloomy byways when he suspended them. He was assisted in this by the fact that the sky had become much lighter and the sun seemed on the verge of appearing above the horizon. He could now see much more of what lay on both sides of the path and could perceive that the one he traveled was only one of a multitude of paths roughly parallel to his. Here and there he could even see solitary and shadowy figures moving on the paths, some in one direction, some in the other.

He might have been tempted to hail one of them, despite his discouraging experience in the hospital, if his attention had not been distracted by a building that had now become clearly visible at what appeared to be a short distance down the path. Unlike the hospital, it had a quite unexceptional appearance, with opaque walls made of what appeared to be bricks. Moreover, its function was obvious; it was a human dwelling place—in particular, a multiunit condominium apartment. Herbert now noticed that he could walk substantially faster and felt less tired. Nevertheless it took much longer to reach the apartment than he had expected, and the sun was well above the horizon by the time he arrived. He saw that the building had an upscale look, and the surrounding grounds were elegantly landscaped with flower gardens and fountains. Also, for the first time, he had a strong sense of recognition. Surely this was a place familiar to him, perhaps one where he had lived in the recent past.

However, this revelation was overshadowed by one even more compelling. The closed door in his memory against which he had earlier pounded in vain now opened of itself. *Fleming!* He was Fleming! He was Herbert Fleming! He had been a scientist, a professor of molecular biology. A legion of memories now arose within him and faded almost at once, but he was able to hold on to his name and title and to the conviction that he had once lived in this apartment building. Moreover, a new flash of memory now informed him that his apartment had been number 423. Yes, of course, 423.

He accordingly walked up to the revolving door that gave access to the lobby. At first he tried crossing the grass, but found it curiously hard to walk on, like stepping on unyielding spikes. He returned to a paved sidewalk, which proved much easier. Through the glass he could see a drowsy security guard furtively smoking a cigarette; the concierge desk was empty. He pushed the revolving door with his hand, but it seemed to be stuck fast. He could not budge it. He then waved at the guard and called out to him, without getting any response. Finally, exasperated, he rushed at the door, thinking to force it open by his momentum, when, to his surprise, he found himself in the lobby. He had passed through effortlessly. If he had been in full possession of his faculties, this would have aroused his interest, but it did not; he was more interested in regaining his room.

Neither the guard nor an early-rising resident passing through the lobby on his way out gave any sign of recognition, although both now seemed somewhat familiar, especially the guard. "Could you let me in my room?" he asked the guard. "I've locked myself out."

Nothing. The guard, who had stood up and hidden his cigarette at the approach of the resident to whom he said an audible "good evening," now sat and resumed smoking. Herbert wondered if he were perhaps asleep and dreaming—or worse—but rejected the idea after feeling his body, which felt as solid and responsive as ever. Certainly, he had been able to hear his own voice. If he could only get back in his own room, perhaps he could sort things out. Meanwhile, the concierge had returned to his desk, but took no more notice of Herbert than the guard.

Evening? Why had the guard said "evening?" One more thing to be sorted out. Herbert went through the motion of pushing the elevator button, but as he was beginning to expect, he could not move it even a millimeter. However, the elevator now arrived on the ground floor of itself, its door opened, and several people emerged and headed for the lobby door. One of them, a fat man in a business suit, would have walked into Herbert if he had not gotten out of the way. Feeling that it would be unwise to attempt the elevator until he was more familiar with the rules of his current existence, he opted for the stairs, which he mounted without difficulty, although the carpet felt stiff and hard under his feet. He found his room and experimentally walked into the door. As in the case of the lobby door, he passed inside easily, although the door remained shut and intact.

Memories now came upon him thick and fast as he recognized one object after another. It was a room appropriate for a gentleman living alone, with a single bedroom, a kitchenette, a bathroom, and a living room. The walls of the latter were lined with bookshelves filled with books, mostly scientific mixed with some classical as well as contemporary novels. He started to reach for a book, stopped upon reflection, and then reached for it anyway; he could not move it, although he could feel its surface.

Nevertheless, there could be no doubt this was his apartment where he had lived for … five years? … Ten? Since … Since when? Since someone had died. But who? He groped in his evolving memory for a name, but nothing came. Perhaps it would come of itself as his own name had. He now noticed a cardboard carton on a small table. The box was filled with what appeared to be framed certificates. He could see only the one on top, which expressed the gratitude of Michelson University for the many years of dedicated service of one Herbert Fleming, together with best wishes for happiness in retirement. He did not bother trying to lift it to see what was underneath.

It occurred to him that bathrooms usually have mirrors, and he walked into it to view his own reflection, not without misgivings. However, he was agreeably surprised. The image that appeared was a substantial improvement over what he had seen in the dimly lit room. What he saw now was an elderly gentleman whose hair and short beard were gray but who was otherwise in reasonably good condition. Indeed, his appearance was respectable and even somewhat distinguished.

Herbert absent-mindedly sat down on the bed, which had not been made lately. It was like sitting on a pile of scrap iron. He got up and walked to the window, where he observed that the sun was about twenty degrees above the horizon. This brought him up short. Something did not make sense. But what? He struggled unsuccessfully to organize his thoughts into coherence and then gave up. Now another discrepancy occurred to him, and he returned to the bathroom and reexamined his image in the mirror. He was wearing a well-fitting pair of slacks and a polo shirt, surely very different from the rumpled and nondescript costume he seemed to remember from his initial reflection. But then, perhaps he was simply mistaken; it had been dark in the room.

There remained the problem of the window and what he had seen through it. However, as he did not know what the problem was, only that there was a problem, there seemed little point in trying to analyze it.

While there seemed little reason to remain in the apartment, it occurred to Herbert that he might at least rest there for a while, although he actually felt less tired than before. Accordingly, he lay down on the floor, which at least was smooth, in preference to the bed. He remained there for some time despite the discomfort, but he did not feel significantly more relaxed or rested.

Finally he got to his feet and looked once more out the window without making any progress in solving the mystery. He then passed once more through the door, down the steps, and through the lobby, which was now fairly crowded with people preparing to leave. He heard many scraps of conversation but did not try to interpret them, although the people's tone suggested that they were leaving for places of entertainment rather than work. On one occasion, he deliberately did not get out of the way as a woman walked toward him, with the result that he was ignominiously pushed aside, as if by an invisible wedge moving with the woman, whose attention he did not attract.

He left the lobby as before, except that this time before trying the door, he made an initial attempt to pass through the wall, which was unsuccessful. Apparently, there were limits to what he could penetrate. He then walked through the door as previously and finally returned to the original path.

After having gone a few paces, he thought of revisiting the lobby briefly to check the time, for his own watch seemed to have stopped. He now made a new discovery; it was impossible to retrace his steps on the path, which he had not attempted before. It was as if an invisible wall existed between where he was and where he had been. His progress down the path was unidirectional. He could stop but could not go back.

Although Herbert thought he had spent only a short time—a half-hour at most—in the apartment, the sun was now high in the sky. And now he recognized what had puzzled him about the view from his window. He now remembered that his window faced west, so he should only have seen the setting sun rather than the rising sun. Nevertheless, the movement of the sun had been opposite to the expected direction. His original puzzlement was now replaced by total bafflement.

Nothing seemed to make any sense. This might have bothered him more if his surroundings had not changed greatly for the better. The risen sun revealed that he was now passing through a landscape of incredible beauty, very different from the desolation he had glimpsed earlier. He seemed to be in a region where glorious gardens filled with yellow daffodils, bluebells, and scarlet tulips alternated with either open fields, where thick grass and purple heather grew, or forests of oak, maple, tulip poplar, and sycamore.

Here and there he saw a sparkling brook. His path crossed one of these by way of a small arched bridge. An occasional red-gold carp grazed the surface. In the distance, on both sides of the path and also at the horizon to which the path headed, he could see mountains—the middle slopes enveloped in mist and the snow-covered peaks bathed in sunlit splendor.

As before, he could see many other paths, running in the same general direction as his own, in the middle distance between his path and the mountains. While a few of these were empty, most held another moving figure, but never more than one. In addition, he could see several groups of what appeared to be very small deer grazing on the lush grass of the open meadows. As he passed by several deer close to the path, one of them raised its head from the grass and appeared to regard Herbert for a moment before returning to his grazing.

This was the closest approach Herbert had achieved to recognition by another seemingly living creature, and he unthinkingly attempted to step off the path and walk toward it. However, the grass was high and unyielding, and he could not get even one foot into it. The deer started and then bounded away, not stopping until they were out of sight. He sighed and resumed walking down the path.

His attention was now totally commanded by a figure moving down the path closest to his own but in a direction opposite to his. It appeared to be a middle-aged woman, walking slowly with lowered eyes, seemingly lost in thought. He recognized her as his daughter Barbara, recollections of whom returned all at once, and yet it was not her. Could this preoccupied and tired-looking woman with the lined forehead and worn features really be Barbara?

"Barbara!" he called, with all the volume he could summon. "It's Dad! Over here!" But he could not penetrate the introspection of the woman, who passed within fifty feet of him before diminishing in the distance. This was nothing new. He had never been able to communicate with Barbara, who had dropped out of college to get married. Several years later she divorced, made a transient return to college, entered into a second marriage (followed by a second divorce), and then became employed in a series of second-rate jobs. However, it was not the unhappy mature woman but the willful and vivacious little girl that he remembered best.

Although he now knew better, he could not forego an attempt to retrace his steps and follow her. The result was the same as before; he could move only one way on his path. The only alternative to moving forward was to remain where he was. After a regretful look at the receding image of Barbara, he resumed his walk. He now had still another problem to contend with. If he could remember Barbara, why could he not remember her mother, to whom he was presumably married? But he knew by now that it was useless to try to force his memory. What he sought would come of itself or not at all.

It seemed as though he had been walking a long time before he sighted another familiar object, although the sun remained at its original position. The extended hike did not tire him. Indeed, he felt stronger and more refreshed than when he started. What he saw was a square stone tower of archaic appearance that gradually became visible, although the building it crowned was obscured by trees. As he drew closer, other towers and spires appeared and finally the buildings themselves. He seemed to be looking at a collection of buildings of Gothic design and of a common collective purpose. He could see many people entering and leaving, most of whom, but not all, were young.

As usual, recognition came all at once. This was the university where he had passed forty years of his life, first as an undergraduate, then, after an interval, as a professor. There was his undergraduate dormitory with its imitation Gothic facade hiding its inner framework of steel girders. Then as now, the overall impression was soothing enough to make one forget the phoniness. There was the lecture hall, where he had taken notes himself and where he had addressed generations of students. It seemed to be only a few steps off the path, and he yielded to the temptation to enter, being careful to stick to the sidewalk. Fortunately, it was the middle of the class and no one was entering or leaving, so he was easily able to mount the steps and walk through the door unimpeded.

He soon found himself standing by the podium beside the current lecturer, who he recognized at once as an erstwhile younger colleague, George Wiley, now well into middle age. From the stage, he looked out over the auditorium, which was almost filled with students. They had not changed; all the familiar types were there. True, the distribution of skin tints was different. Whereas once he would have seen little but Caucasian greyish-pink, now they were often black, brown, yellowish, or the off-white of the Middle East. But the back row was still populated by sullen individuals who spent much time whispering to each other, while the front seats contained eager and compulsive note-takers, with a high proportion of East Asians.

Here was where one found the pre-meds and those aiming for the "prestigious" graduate schools. There in the front row was a lean and intense student wearing a yarmulke, taking notes with furious concentration. Next to him sat an even more dedicated Korean, who seemed to be transcribing verbatim every word the lecturer spoke. On the other side of the Korean was a hard-faced black with a penetrating stare, whose attention was likewise totally focused upon the lecture.

"Don't overdo it," he wanted to cry out to them. "Have a little fun too, while you can." But not everyone in the audience was committed. Here and there in the auditorium he could see a bored-looking student, aloof to everything and lost in reverie. He noticed on one of these the dark shadows under the eyes, the meaning of which he knew so well.

His attention was now drawn from the student audience to the lecture itself. Wiley happened to be dealing with a topic central to Herbert's own research. While his exposition fitted Herbert's findings in broad outline, there was some divergence in detail, and in one instance there was total disagreement. What was worse, there was no mention of Herbert Fleming. The credit was given entirely to others.

Herbert's mood now abruptly shifted to cold rage, compounded by frustration. "You fool, you've got it all wrong! You don't know what you're talking about! You always were a silly ass!" he yelled at the speaker without the slightest effect. His rage subsided as quickly as it arose. What difference did it make after all? His work was a part—a significant part—of the building structure of knowledge. By humanity's great good fortune, there were too many scientists for posterity to remember their names. "I'm sorry, George," he said to no one. "I didn't mean it."

Herbert had observed that as long as he was off the path in an accessible enclave, such as the present one, he could move freely in any direction. He now decided to capitalize on this to visit his old laboratory, which had been the real focus of his academic career. This presented some difficulty, as that part of the campus had been extensively modified.

When he attempted to walk to where he thought the building should be, he found that, instead of a well-defined structure like the lecture hall, he seemed to see a blur, as of two buildings trying to occupy the same space. Sometimes one image predominated; sometimes the other. He found that if he focused his attention upon one of these, he could attenuate the other somewhat, so that he could recognize the older building in which his laboratory had been situated. But if he relaxed his concentration for a moment, the illusion vanished and the blurred chimerical structure returned. When he stepped into the blurred image, he found himself in a total chaos, reminiscent of the hospital he had passed through earlier.

Clearly it was hopeless to try to locate his old laboratory in this mess. Accordingly, he left the building and walked in the direction he felt the path should be. He was relieved to see that the buildings he now passed had a well-defined and normal appearance, with only minor blurring confined to a few details. He had learned to stay on paved areas and soon regained the path. He had only one troubling experience. While crossing a street, he conscientiously used the pedestrian crossing, paying insufficient attention to an oncoming car, which ran right through him without even slowing down. However, he was merely thrust aside undamaged.

He was now beginning to understand the rules. He could not occupy the same space as a solid material object. The only exception was a door he had been accustomed to using in the past. If he walked into such a closed door, he passed in one quantum jump to the other side of the door. If a moving object collided with him, it pushed him out of its space, again in a discontinuous way. If he stepped on grass, it refused to bend and excluded him from its space.

He was back on the path now. The sun was directly overhead. He walked quite vigorously now; the stiffness and exhaustion he had felt earlier were entirely gone. He traveled through a region of rolling hills, while the mountains toward which the path led seemed much larger and closer.

What lay in the intervening distance was at first concealed by the hills, but finally he rounded a curve and saw before him a collection of single-family homes. These were in mock-colonial style and placed on half-acre lots. One of them not far from the path drew him at once. A dispassionate observer might have declared it similar in all essential respects to the others and part of a subset, whose identical members were spaced discreetly well apart. Nevertheless, it had an emotional impact upon Herbert not shared by the others. He accordingly left the path and walked toward the very ordinary brick dwelling with the portico and four meaningless pillars. He was glad to see that the image was perfectly sharp; apparently the house had not been modified.

As he walked up the sidewalk leading to the front door, recollections now came very fast. Here was where he had lived for twenty years. He had moved in with the wonderful girl he had married, only she had turned out to be not so wonderful after all. Here Barbara had passed her childhood and adolescence before going on to college. There was a tricycle on the front lawn; could it be Barbara's? No, don't be silly, and anyway there was another little girl coming to ride it. He liked the little girl. She had a friendly and happy look, and he would have said hello to her if he could.

Herbert walked through the front door and into the foyer. His old study was only a few steps away on his right. The floor-to-ceiling bookshelves he had installed were still there and still filled with books, but of a different kind, although still technical. These books were mostly about computer hardware and software. Perhaps their owner was a programmer or electronic engineer. There was a leather armchair in a corner, much like his own, where he had conceived and analyzed most of his work.

He left the study and walked into the living room. The pegged oak floor, which Ella had never liked, was now covered with wall-to-wall carpeting. He noticed a mirror over the fireplace mantel and walked up to it to view himself. What he now saw was a youngish man in his late twenties or early thirties with a full head of hair and no beard. Still. it was unmistakably the same man whose reflections he had seen earlier.

"It's as if I were going through life backward," he thought. "But what comes next?"

At this moment, he heard women's voices coming from the direction of the family room. Upon walking to the source of the sound he found two women sitting on a sofa and conversing. One of them, who was plump, seemed to be the current mistress of the house and the other, who was thin, a recently acquired neighbor.

"This house has quite a history," said the plump woman.

"Yes, I've heard about it," said the other. "Isn't this where a woman who was caught embezzling money killed herself?"

"That's right. She took it from a charity where she worked. Apparently her husband wasn't in on it. She took an overdose of sleeping pills, but something went wrong and she stayed in a coma for five years."

"It sounds terrible," said the thin woman.

"It was."

"There was more to it than that," thought Herbert. "Much more."

Ella had stolen the money to pay off a massive gambling debt she had run up without Herbert's knowledge. She had been a singularly inept thief and had been easily caught. The woman's words had aroused neither anger nor sorrow. He was past both emotions, having been drained of both during the hideous five years the woman had alluded to and that he now remembered so well. Meanwhile, the two women continued their chat. They both looked so complacent he could have struck them.

Herbert had no desire to remain further in the house. He turned and retraced his steps, walking through the front door, down the sidewalk, and back to the path. The sun was now in his eyes, and the mountains seemed very close. He must have been longer in the house than he thought, but then time seemed to be very irregular lately. His walking speed must have increased, for when he looked back after what seemed like a short interval, the suburb and its houses were already out of sight.

His attention was now drawn to the mountains directly ahead and, in particular, to their forested lower slopes into which the path disappeared. There was no sign of any pass. He could already see that the deciduous oaks, maples, and tulip poplars that populated the lowest levels were replaced higher up by pines and other evergreens, and then by rock, and finally by snow. However would he get through that? But go through he must, unless he wished to remain where he was.

Herbert now observed that as the upward slope of the path became significant, it also ceased to be linear and began to wind about the foothills of the mountains. He could no longer see far ahead and was thus surprised, upon rounding a curve, to see a stationary human figure about sixty yards ahead who was looking in his direction and seemingly awaiting him. What was still more startling was that the man obviously saw him and walked to meet him. As the distance between them diminished, he had time to observe his unexpected companion closely. What he saw was reassuring, although somewhat puzzling.

He saw what appeared to be a robust man in early middle age, dressed in an archaic costume, with boots and a curious conical hat, rather reminiscent of stock portrayals of Puritan settlers in early New England. However, the very English face was open, frank, and friendly.

"Have no fear, friend," he said. "I mean no harm and have come to guide you the rest of the way."

"How is it that you can see and hear me while no one else can?" asked Herbert.

"You and I share the same world, whereas we are only onlookers in the other world," answered the stranger, whose accent was strange but perfectly intelligible.

"Does this mean I am dead?" asked Herbert.

"No," said the stranger, "not yet. But it does mean that I am dead."

The two walked side by side, and Herbert had the opportunity to examine his new companion more closely. His initial impression of seventeenth-century clothing was confirmed, as was that of gracious kindness which was reflected by an unassuming smile.

"Who are you?" asked Herbert.

The stranger's smile broadened, and his eyes twinkled.

"You would have heard of me," he said. "In life I bore the name of John Bunyan."

Herbert stared at him silently for a moment. "Are you the author of …?" He could not recall the name of the famous book, a flawless work of art that he had not read or thought of since early adolescence.

"The same," said Bunyan. "Who is better fitted to guide you than I?"

"Who indeed," said Herbert. "I loved your book." As he began to recall details, he added, "but I did not agree with everything in it."

"Nor do I," said Bunyan. "I got many things wrong, as mortals often do."

"But why," asked Herbert, "would such a man as you trouble himself with an insignificant person like me?"

This produced a burst of merriment in Bunyan, which began as a chuckle and ended as a deep resonant laugh that seemed to come from his innermost being.

"I am the best judge of that," he said finally. "Come, let us dispatch. Our time grows short." And indeed the sun was now in the lowest quadrant of the sky. They walked quite rapidly now. When Herbert turned his head to look behind him, he saw that they had attained a considerable height, although he could still see the path on the plain far below.

Herbert did not feel at all tired now, although they had been climbing a steep gradient for some time. As the day waned and they proceeded farther into the mountains, the recollections of his past life, which had so preoccupied him earlier, became hazy and unreal and finally ceased altogether. His mental perceptions had also changed, and he no longer wondered at his strange situation or doubted the likelihood of his passing through it intact. Perhaps his altered outlook prevented him from being disturbed by the progressive shrinkage of his size relative to Bunyan. While they had originally been of similar heights, he now barely came up to his guide's armpits.

"Where are we going?" Herbert asked. If he had retained his normal faculties, he would have been surprised that his voice was now an octave higher in pitch. Bunyan gave him an amused look

"Did they not teach you anything?" he asked.

But now Herbert's attention was diverted by what he saw and heard farther up the mountain. It was now twilight, and ahead he could make out what seemed to be a vast collection of lights, some stationary, some flickering. He could also hear a kind of murmuring, as if from a collection of voices singing far away. He felt a great joy and desire to join them and rushed ahead toward the glorious light, feeling as if he were dwindling to nothing and growing to enormous size at the same time.

In real time, Barbara Fleming sat on a sofa in the hospital lounge, trying to sleep.

It was four o'clock in the morning, and there was only one other visitor in the lounge, a morose-looking, baldheaded man who never spoke and seemed totally submerged in his own concerns.

However, she was still awake when the nurse came to tell her that her father was already dead.

"He died in his sleep. He never regained consciousness or showed the slightest sign of life. He was lucky. It was an easy, peaceful death."

The news had not hit Barbara yet. Soon there would be a burst of grief, but for now, she felt mostly relief.

"I never really knew him, and now I never will."

"I'm a believer, and I think there will be a reunion."

"I wish I were."

And then the grief Barbara had held off hit her all at once and very hard. She suffered for three days, but on the fourth she awoke feeling at peace and happier than she had for a long time.

ROUND TRIP

Along with the other crew members, Kevin Patrig was awakened from his long, dreamless sleep in gradual stages extending over several days terrestrial time. His body temperature was slowly raised to its former value, and his system was freed from the drugs that had retarded his metabolism, avoided tissue damage, and helped to minimize aging. The process was, of course, mediated and carefully monitored by computer-controlled devices that needed only very general human supervision. While this went on, the velocity of the space vehicle slowed from a significant fraction of the speed of light to a value more suitable for reentry into a planetary atmosphere. As Patrig's brain began functioning again, he left his fetus-like sleep and began to dream actively. At first his dreams were bland and harmless, but later they became more serious and threatening. The menace was never seen clearly, but it inspired dread, and its faceless presence pursued Patrig down endless dark corridors and trails in a sinister forest.

His awakening was abrupt, and he found himself looking into the nondescript face of Cermak, who was bending over him. It had been Cermak's watch that had occupied about six months of terrestrial time. To Patrig's surprise, he saw that the entire crew was awake, including Captain Tsao, who summoned them to a meeting in the spacecraft's tiny conference room. He was bewildered by this, as he knew they could not have possibly arrived at their destination.

The others were as confused as he was, and the room grew very quiet as Tsao began to speak. He was a rather handsome man of the north Chinese type, with an intelligent and humorous face. His remarks were brief and to the point:

"As you may have surmised, there has been a change in plans. There has been a partial power failure, which precludes our reaching Leonardo V. We have accordingly returned to the solar system and will be landing on Earth in a few months' terrestrial time."

There was a moment's silence, which was broken by Lopez, a short swarthy man with Mediterranean features.

"So everything's blown then?"

"In a word, yes. This is a possibility we were all warned about and chose to disregard. It could have been worse—much worse. As there was not much for you to do, we decided to let the rest of you sleep until you were needed."

"Who are *we*?"

"Topolsky, Cermak, and me. The problem was recognized on Topolsky's watch. He roused me, and I woke up Cermak. We've been alternating watches."

"How far did we get?" asked Abiola, a light-skinned black, who wore a perpetual expression of "this requires some thought."

"Not very. Only about ten light years."

"How much terrestrial time has elapsed?" asked Patrig. The room grew very quiet. All the murmuring ceased.

"About forty years."

It was roughly what they had expected, but it still came as a shock. It would be some time before it really hit them. One man sighed audibly. One of the three spacewomen shook her head as if trying to awake from a bad dream.

So there it was. Earth's first manned space probe to a putative planetary system had ended in a nonevent, canceling out years of hard work and hopelessly disrupting their lives. Forty years. What would they be coming back to? Such an Enoch Arden situation was a cliché in certain literary genres, but was, mercifully, exceedingly rare in real life. But now Captain Tsao began again. At first he dealt with technical details of the power failure, but then he turned to matters of even more general interest.

"You will recall that for obvious reasons, our periodic communications with our terrestrial base had to be confined to very broad summaries of events. In particular, no attempt would be made to inquire after, or communicate with, personal contacts. As of right now, your surviving relatives and acquaintances are still assuming that they will never see you again."

That rang true enough. Even if a return had been planned after they reached their goal, many generations would have elapsed. Tsao continued,

"Perhaps you have some curiosity about what has been going on these last forty years?"

"I can't help feeling a lively interest," said Lopez. There was no sign of dissent from the others.

"Very well. Actually, there have been surprisingly few unexpected changes. The political, economic, and demographic trends that you remember have continued unabated. While it does not bother me, some of you might be disturbed to learn that thirty percent of the population of the United States is now Asian, mostly Chinese and Indian. Economically, the country has finally pretty well recovered from the great stock market crash of 2020 and the following depression. The last of the so-called *baby boomers*, whose retirement caused it all, have nearly all died off."

"Good riddance," said Cermak. Tsao nodded, but said nothing. The others were silent too. The depression had been a factor in the decision of many of them to volunteer.

"Who's president now?" asked Patrig. He was a muscular, clean-cut man, with eyes as blue as a Bunsen burner flame.

"His name is Gonzalez."

"About time," said Lopez.

"Don't get your hopes up. Actually, he's half Chinese."

"Oh, and by the way," said Tsao, "there is a real world government now and one global currency, but it's still based on the dollar. There's only one global army."

Several men cursed audibly. Someone softly uttered the word "shit." Tsao shrugged.

"That's the way it is. While English is still the language of government, commerce, and technology everywhere, it's rapidly losing ground to Spanish and Chinese at home."

The orientation continued for some time, but Patrig's mind had wandered. He wondered about many things. What would he do now? He would have lost his place in line for a space expedition, and his technical knowledge would be forty years behind the times. It was little consolation to learn that two new voyages to Leonardo V had departed since they left, and one of these was over halfway there.

Tsao now broke into his thoughts with an announcement that compelled his attention:

"Perhaps the most visible change you will notice is that there are significantly fewer people. Trends like family limitation and feminism have spread from European and American whites to all ethnic groups. These, plus a steadily aging population and a sharp rise in the death rate during the depression, when malnutrition was common, have resulted in a surplus of deaths over births for many years. Something like this occurred in Russia in the late twentieth century. The population of what was the United States is now only about 320 million, many of them elderly. The median age is about fifty. You will see few children."

The implications of this were too much for Kevin to grasp at once, and he returned to his own private musings. Most of all, he wondered about Laura and whether she was still among the living and whether he should try to find her. Perhaps she would find him; the news of their return would surely be all over the media. But why should she? They had never married, and she had given him his freedom, although she obviously had done so reluctantly. She would surely have married long ago or at least paired off with someone else.

But who else could he contact? His father had died long before he left, having killed himself during the sequel to the 2020 crash. His mother had been in her sixties and in poor health. He had no siblings. He had always been somewhat of a loner with no really close friends, except of course for Laura.

They had met while in college, before he committed himself to a career as a spaceman. From the start it had been a somewhat one-sided love affair. He was of much more central importance to Laura than she was to him. He had been flattered to be the object of single-minded devotion, which was becoming rare, even from so ordinary a person as Laura.

Ordinary she certainly was. Although it had been only a few weeks in his own time frame since he had last seen her, his inner visualization of her was already a little blurred. She was a petite brunette, two years older than himself, with a wistful and careworn look that made her seem older yet. Perhaps it was the aura of wistful dependency that had drawn him to her in the first place. Assuredly, it was not her conversation, which was as unremarkable as her appearance. Nevertheless, she had stuck with him through the grueling two years of astronaut school. The rigor of this was not justified by what they would actually be doing and may have served primarily to reduce the swarm of aspiring spacemen to a manageable number.

He had never regretted moving in with her. It had meant reliable meals, clean and orderly surroundings, and freedom from sexual tensions. He had been only a middling student and was far down the priority list that determined who would be chosen for actual missions. He had therefore been compelled to spend five years in the reserves with only a small stipend, not enough to live on, which was balanced by the requirement for periodic training sessions. During this time he had basically been supported by Laura, whose earnings as a laboratory technician were supplemented by his own in a series of small, part-time jobs. Jobs were not plentiful in the post-crash years, which partially explained the popularity of the spaceman program.

Laura had never pressed him to get married or to get a full-time job, although she would obviously have been glad of either. Both were hard to reconcile with his five-year commitment to the space reserves, with the possibility of being summoned to a mission at any time. While he had, of course, the option of refusing, that would have meant refunding both his scholarship and the cumulative sum of his reservist stipends.

Formal marriage he had never seriously considered either, although Laura had been the equivalent of a wife for some time, including the fact that he was somewhat bored with her. He had temporized, saying that they would get married as soon as his five-year commitment was over if he was not called up. As time passed it had seemed less and less likely that he would find a mission before his time was up. Indeed, by comparing his rate of movement up the priority list with the time remaining, he had felt that he could almost discard the possibility.

It had come therefore as somewhat of a shock when, after three and a half years, he was summoned to a mission. Obviously he had been jumped ahead, presumably because of deaths or resignations. Laura had seemingly taken the news well at first, and their final weeks together had been by far the best. Their lovemaking in particular had assumed a poignancy and urgency it had lacked before. On their penultimate day, he had told her to consider him henceforth as dead and to find a new lover and hopefully a husband. She had not answered but looked very sad and rushed outside for a long walk. There had been no love making that night, and when he woke up the next morning, she was gone. He had thought of calling her at work but decided against it. Better this way.

Tsao broke into his thoughts again.

"We will be docking at the new Hermann Minkowski Space Center, which is not far from Dallas."

There was a subdued murmur.

"Who the hell was Hermann Minkowski?"

"I dunno. Must have been since our time."

"Perhaps it might help to think of it this way," said Tsao. "Our space voyage turned out to be a round trip, but we are history's first authentic time travelers. We have leapfrogged over forty years of terrestrial time, thanks to relativity and cryobiology, without its leaving a mark on us biologically. However, you should be aware that your immunities may have suffered, and you may be more vulnerable to the new viruses and bacteria that have probably appeared in the last forty years. But because you were freed from all microorganisms before you left, you will not present any danger to others."

Although it had been explained to him many times and he had accepted it as an arcane fact, Kevin never really understood why velocities approaching the speed of light retarded aging. "It's not as if you're getting something for nothing. Actually, you're losing something, namely, a biological process to which you would normally be entitled."

It did not help, and Kevin's thoughts returned to their interrupted pattern.

If Laura were still alive, she would be in her late sixties now, over twice his biological age. Small brunettes did not wear well, and she could probably be mistaken for his mother now. She was probably married with two or three grown children, perhaps some grandchildren. Moreover, while he was hardly returning as a failure, neither could he be considered a hero. Indeed, he had done nothing at all, not even age, for forty years of her time.

Nevertheless, the more his common sense discouraged him from contacting Laura, the more he felt drawn to the idea. Finally, he decided to postpone his decision until he was back on Earth. This was easy to do, as all crew members had their hands full during the final weeks of the voyage. He was glad of this, for it kept him from dwelling on his condition and prospects. He could not, however, avoid contact with the others and, in particular, having to listen to their plans for the future, which in comparison seemed elaborate and promising. Most of them had taken advantage of the liberal long-term insurance policies offered by the Space Agency against just this eventuality. They could afford to be generous as the likelihood of ever having to pay was slight. Several should in fact be rich men. He cursed himself for not having taken advantage of this.

The closer they approached the end of their voyage, the slower time seemed to pass and the more restless they became. Several of the crew members seemed to retreat into themselves, saying little to anyone. Quarrels now broke out over trivia.

"If you didn't mean it, then what the fuck didja say it for?"

Finally they docked at the Minkowski Space Center, where they were subjected to a week of medical testing, debriefing, and orientation, all in a sterile environment. The debriefing was little more than a formality. It basically confirmed what Captain Tsao had already told them, and the physical examination verified the effectiveness of the procedures for arresting metabolism and aging. Spaceman Kevin Patrig was indeed essentially the same healthy twenty-five-year-old he had been when he left earth forty terrestrial years earlier. Actually, his biological age could be anywhere from twenty-five to thirty but certainly not more than that.

He was officially notified that his obligation to the erstwhile Space Agency, which had been incorporated into the International Space Authority, was now satisfied and he would be given his terminal pay, which he chose to receive as a lump sum. Nothing was said about any pension. A Dr. Ramachandran, an exceedingly dark Indian, delivered the medical lecture to the entire group. He was clad in a kind of sterile spacesuit.

"I cannot impress upon you too strongly the importance of renewing your immunizations. You have doubtless heard of how most of the original American Indians were wiped out by European diseases, to which they had no immunity. You are in a similar situation. You will be entering a biomedical world that is very different from the one you left. Many microorganisms that were formerly con-fined to remote locations have spread all over the globe. In addition, new strains developed for biological warfare are present. Also, even for wild type species, mutations are occurring constantly. There are some species that can kill you within twenty-four hours.

"This is not all. As you are aware, your own microorganisms were eliminated before you left on the space journey. This means that your own immunological defense systems have been inactive for forty years, with consequences that are unknown to us, as there is no precedent."

"How long will it take?" asked Lopez.

"About six months. We can't give you all the injections at once; it might kill you."

"Is it compulsory?" asked Patrig.

"No, we cannot force you. If you decline, you will be hurting no one but yourself. If you do, you will have to sign a release, absolving the Authority of all responsibility."

The others were shocked at learning that Patrig was going to skip the course of immunizations.

"Don't be a fool." "They don't have to do this." "It's free." "What have you got to lose?"

"What I have to lose is six more months of my life. Thanks but no thanks. I'll take my chances and I'm not signing no release."

He had expected a strong reaction to his decision and that strenuous efforts would be made to dissuade him. Actually, there was no reaction at all—almost as if they didn't care very much.

He was neither surprised nor disappointed at the absence of any formal recep-tion or official welcome. He had been prepared for that by the minor attention given their return by the media and by the absence of any official pronouncements. He did see several reporters talking to Tsao but other than that, nothing. The authorities were clearly very modest about the first Leonardo V mission; the news of its failure would be many years old now. The America he had known was gone, and the new America no longer took a chauvinistic interest in such things.

And, after all, they hadn't done shit.

He spent the first few days after leaving the sterile enclosure in a nearby guest house for space personnel. He spent the time filling out a lengthy questionnaire about the voyage. This was a condition for receiving the stipend. The other guests, who were mostly Chinese or Korean, looked at him curiously but did not talk much. By the end of his stay, he began to show symptoms like those of a common cold, but nothing to worry about.

The Minkowski Center was not far from San Antonio, where he had lived until a few weeks ago in biological time. He thought of renting a surface vehicle but remembered that his license was forty years out of date. He sighed and boarded a train of advanced design that, at four hundred kilometers per hour, took only an hour and a half to reach San Antonio. The landscape was quite as dull as he remembered and did not distract him from observing his fellow passengers. He was almost the sole non-Hispanic white in the car. Of the three other exceptions, two were elderly. He noticed that several passengers cast occasional curious glances in his direction. His appearance must have been somewhat dated, although he had been provided with a new suit of clothes, courtesy of the Space Authority. No one wore mustaches or cross-cropped hair anymore, not even the military.

Despite what he had been told, he was surprised by the appearance of San Antonio. It had always been a somewhat slow-moving town, but he had expected some visible growth and change. Not only had there been little recent construction, but there was also a large number of razed and boarded-up buildings. This would fit with the national and worldwide drop in population. Moreover, virtually all signs were now in Spanish, as were most of the snatches of conversation he heard on the streets. This was not all. Not only were there fewer people, but they were also older. The progressive aging of the ethnic European population, which had become noticeable even before he left, seemed now to have extended to other groups.

After checking in at the moderately priced Zapata Hotel, he went to his old bank, where he established an account and deposited his severance paycheck. Except for one now-quite-old lady who did not remember him, all the tellers were new since his time and Spanish-speaking. There was no sign saying "Se habla Espanol." That would have been redundant. As it was only midafternoon and he had plenty of time, he decided to walk the ten blocks back to his hotel. What he saw only confirmed and strengthened the impressions derived from his initial taxi ride through town. While traffic was much lighter than he remembered, the appearance of the automobiles had not greatly changed, although the proportion of electric and hydrogen-powered vehicles was substantially larger. Indeed, petrochemical users were obviously becoming scarce. Perhaps this accounted for the improved characteristics of the atmosphere, which seemed amazingly clear and fresh, while the sky was an intense blue. This was definitely a plus and somewhat improved his spirits. He also noticed several vending machines dispensing marijuana cigarettes.

Nevertheless, he found little to cheer him on his walk back to the hotel. It would have been an exaggeration to say that San Antonio was now a ghost city, but that would have been closer to the truth than to call it a normal, lively metropolis. Where were the tour buses packed with visitors? Where were the window shoppers? Where were the sidewalk kiosks filled with all kinds of publications? Above all, where were the young people? In the course of his walk, he had seen only a few people of his own biological age. It was at this time that he began to show signs of serious illness, as his common cold-like symptoms grew rapidly worse.

When he was back in his hotel room, he at first tried unsuccessfully to take a nap before supper. Then he got up abruptly, went to the audiovisual device, and entered his old ID number. The screen remained dark and then displayed an error message. He then requested a search, first local and then national, for Laura Duncan or Laura Patrig. The local search drew a blank; the national search identified six Laura Duncans and eight Laura Patrigs. He went through the lists one by one. Only three of the Duncans and two of the Patrigs were home, and the images that appeared on the screen could not possibly be whom he was seeking. He excused himself in each case and resolved to try again later, but without much hope.

It occurred to him to try the police, but he could not find a listing for them. An inquiry to the desk brought the response:

"Senor, San Antonio has not had an independent police force for years. There is no need for one. I suggest you try the regional office in Dallas."

Of course. Few young people, little crime. He remembered now that he had not seen a single policeman since he arrived.

Although he had little appetite and was in fact beginning to feel increasingly ill, with a mild fever, he forced himself to get down a few bites of a dull Mexican-style dinner in the hotel's dining room. He also studied a map of San Antonio's new subway system, noting that one stop was within a half mile of the modest, Iberian-style, tile-roofed townhouse where he had lived with Laura. After dinner he went for another random walk, in the course of which he passed what seemed to be a singles bar, hesitated for a moment, and then entered, although he rarely drank and never drank alone. The clientele was mostly middle-aged, swarthy, and Spanish-speaking and he stood out. He found a place at the bar and ordered a vodka and tonic, feeling all the while the center of curious, although not hostile, attention.

He was almost through his drink when a somewhat younger woman who seemed different from the other customers approached. She was blond and rather pretty, with a pleasant smile, and when she said "hello," her voice was husky but without an accent. Perhaps things were looking up. He noticed, however, that derisive smiles appeared on several of the customers. Still, he had been about to answer when he observed that his new acquaintance had an Adam's apple and a masculine set of the shoulders. He turned away, paid for his drink, and walked out, hearing behind him a murmur of laughter. "Some things never change," he thought.

When he resumed his walk, he was hit by an overwhelming desire to see Laura again under any conditions. It was a categorical imperative, unanswerable and far stronger than anything he had felt in his old terrestrial life. But this was impossible. His Laura did not exist. Even if he located her, all he would find would be an elderly stranger. Nothing but grief could come out of pursuing this. To complicate matters, he was now beginning to feel quite sick and obviously had a substantial fever.

Clearly, he had made a mistake in not staying for the immunizations. Common sense would dictate that he return to his room and go to bed. But common sense is vulnerable to almost any temptation. He would put the idea out of his thoughts, only to have it return unbidden and stronger than ever. This happened several times. Finally it became unendurable. He found himself walking back to a subway station he remembered having passed earlier. When he arrived, he was covered with a clammy sweat and his fingers trembled slightly as he put a bill in the slot and collected his change and a ticket to his old neighborhood.

The last forty years had not been kind to Santana Street. While it was still largely lined with tile-roofed townhouses, they now had a battered look, and there were gaps here and there. Many were boarded up, and broken windows appeared occasionally, even among those still occupied. The grass in many of the small lawns was tall and there were many weeds. It was a clear and warm night. When he was last here, there would have been many people on the porches, drinking iced tea or beer and chatting. Now there were not many people about, and most of the windows were dark. He noticed, with some apprehension, that the sky had clouded over and there was a feel of rain in the air. Superimposed upon his illness, he was, to his surprise, beginning to feel his rapidly consumed drink. Forty years of abstinence seemed to have undermined his resistance to alcohol.

It was with a feeling of dread that he approached his old address. He half hoped it would be burned down or demolished. The street numbers marched relentlessly by: 5401, 5403, 5405, 5407 ... And there it was—5409. While the house seemed reasonably intact, it did not give the impression of being occupied. There were no visible lights, no car parked in front, and the grass was tall. Finally, there was an old-fashioned mailbox, with a faded label saying "Mrs. Carmen Perez."

"So much for this cockamamie idea," he thought. "I may as well go back." By this time he was beginning to feel quite sick and somewhat muddled.

But he found himself walking up the steps to the door, pressing the doorbell, which did not work, and then knocking. He knocked three times and then, after an interval, four more. As he had expected, there was no response from the house. He felt very tired and weak, so much so that he sat down on the steps to rest for a moment.

He was trying to summon strength for the walk back to the subway stop when he saw a taxi and hailed it. The driver was off duty but agreed to take him back to his hotel for an extortionate price. Somehow he made his way inside the hotel and into the elevator, ignoring the stares of the desk clerk and concierge, who saw his flushed face and staggering gait and thought he was drunk.

Common sense should have told him to get himself to an emergency room or at least call a doctor, but he was too exhausted to do anything but lie down. He lapsed into unconsciousness almost at once and entered a strange but pleasant dream.

He seemed to be preparing to enter an elegant suburban house with a well-cared-for lawn. He knew that it was his own house and that Laura was waiting for him inside, the way one does in dreams. When he went inside, he saw an elderly lady with snowy white hair and an expression of kindly benevolence.

He and Laura were together again and on equal terms. She had not become young again; rather, he had grown older, so that they were now of similar ages. They were in a large house, in which he sensed the presence of grown children and many grandchildren. It seemed to be some kind of holiday or celebration, for a large table had been set and a beaming Laura had come to summon them to dinner.

Then he noticed a banner across the top of the door. It read "WELCOME HOME, SPACEMAN!" The celebration was in his honor. He heard children running and the slower steps of their parents.

His body was found in bed early the next morning by the hotel chambermaid. He was taken by ambulance to the nearest hospital emergency room, where he was pronounced dead on arrival. The cause of death was established to be Krakauer's Syndrome, a fast-acting pulmonary infection originating in African chimpanzees, which had become widespread in America in the last decade. Since no living relatives could be located, the International Space Authority was kind enough to make funds available for a burial plot in Arlington National Cemetery. He was given a military funeral, which was attended by only a handful of functionaries and a lone elderly woman who stood outside the circle of graveside mourners. Long after the others left, Mrs. Carmen Perez knelt and placed a single white rose on Kevin Patrig's grave.

978-1-58348-480-7
1-58348-480-9

12-07
10.95

DATE

FEB 0 4 2008	
MAY 3 0 2008	
APR 2 1 2016	

DEMCO 38-296

Printed in the United States
94661LV00002B/399/A